Wicked and Whimsical

Kathleen Fernandes

Wicked and Whimsical

Thanks

I would like to thank the Women Writers' Network
for their advice, critique and encouragement

To my parents for entrusting me with a sense of humour
and a set of principles to live by

Wicked and Whimsical
ISBN 978 1 76041 958 5
Copyright © text Kathleen Fernandes 2020
Cover image: Kayla Maurais from Unsplash

First published 2020 by
GINNINDERRA PRESS
PO Box 3461 Port Adelaide 5015
www.ginninderrapress.com.au

Contents

Deceptive

She had almost backed out at the last minute. Miranda used to think that only desperates ever answered singles ads. She hadn't told anyone, not even her workmates. Their whispers and nudges didn't bear contemplating.

Perry was very talkative. He hadn't stopped since they'd met at the outdoor café. She studied him as she lit a cigarette. He was on the podgy side and needed a haircut. He coughed. Was that his polite way of telling her to refrain? Perhaps.

She twisted strands of her hair and wondered whether her ex still ironed his ties. Relationships became a bore if you clung to the same person too long. When they'd split, acquaintances still asked Miranda about her other half, as though she couldn't possibly exist on her own. Other half. What a joke.

'Julie's terrific,' he said.

'Julie?' asked Miranda, sitting upright. Did he already have a girlfriend?

He continued as though he hadn't heard her. 'She's just so smooth all over and there's never any arguments either. It's great being able to practise on her.' He grinned.

Miranda nearly choked on her coffee.

'Are you okay?' He leaned forward.

'Yes, yes, I'm fine.' What the hell did he mean by practise on her?

Two children and their mother walked passed. One of the children vaulted into a nearby puddle.

'Now, why did you do that, darling?' crooned the mother.

Her darling didn't answer. Miranda was thankful she'd never had children.

'Yes, Julie's very special.' He poured himself a Coke.

If she's so special, why are you here wasting my time?' mused Miranda.

'So, is Julie your um…girlfriend?'

'No,' He took a sip of Coke.

'Well, who is she then?' Miranda, irritated, lit another cigarette.

'She's my doll.'

'Your what!' She stared at his fingers. Those fleshy white fingers with the manicured nails had fondled the doll. His doll. She wanted to spew.

Suddenly, she remembered having read a case about the unusual death of a middle-aged man. He had suffered a heart attack after making love to an inflatable rubber doll. How sick. She drained her coffee. Perry didn't look the type to frequent shops that stocked accessories for the licentious. But you couldn't always tell by appearances. Perhaps the doll was a substitute for his loneliness. Some substitute.

She was curious as to whether his friends knew about Julie. That's if he had any. Was he always so revealing on a first date?

'Anything wrong?' He rapped his fingers on the table. His nails were cleaner than her own.

'No, of course not.' She found it hard to swallow.

'You've gone very quiet.'

She glanced at her watch. 'I'll have to go soon.'

Perry laid a hand over hers. 'Don't go yet. We're just getting to know each other.'

She pulled her hand away.

He shrugged, 'You know how I was telling you earlier about me working in a department store…'

She couldn't, but nodded. What was coming next? 'Look, I really have to go.'

'Wait. Let me finish. My boss gave me a promotion. I'm now a trained window dresser. Julie was a present. The boss said I could have her, as they had too many store dummies.'

Miranda sighed and reclined in her chair. What a relief. And she thought he was a real pervert. Perry might even become tempting if he lost some weight and got himself a decent haircut. She could offer to do it. Her ex used to say she was an ace with the scissors, that was until she slashed all his ties. Had it only been six months since the break-up. She'd had enough of celibacy.

He glanced at the menu. 'I'm starving.'

'So am I,' said Miranda.

'Thought you had to go.'

'Changed my mind. Can't wait to meet Julie.'

Exit Left

Friday nights had become a routine. A five-year routine. Zoe would call at Lina's unit with a sponge cake and ice cream, while Lina supplied the wine, cheese and crackers. Both women were single and in their late thirties. Despite their friendship, Lina was becoming more exasperated with Zoe's spineless attitude and her inability to confront her domineering mother.

'I'm standing up to her now,' Zoe had said once after a few glasses of wine.

'Like hell you are!' Lina didn't believe her. 'How are you ever going to get out? Live your life? Meet anyone?'

'But Lina, my mother is sick. She needs me. I'm the only one she's got since Dad died.'

'Zoe, you're nearly forty. You've never even had a boyfriend, for God's sake! Your mother is just a selfish old bitch.'

Theirs was a worn conversation. Zoe's reaction was predictable. She winced and then shrugged.

Inspecting the table, Lina hoped it would meet with her friend's approval. There was a bottle of wine, a bowl of black olives, plate of crackers and a wedge of ricotta cheese. A sealed packet of party picks was next to the green serviettes. Zoe didn't like green. She preferred lemon.

'But you don't eat the bloody serviettes. What's the difference?' Lina had snapped at the time. She would never understand her. If she wasn't arguing over the colour of the serviettes, she'd be arguing over the wine not being chilled enough. Lina wondered why she bothered to make the effort. Zoe didn't seem to appreciate anything.

It was six-thirty by the kitchen wall clock. She'd be arriving any minute. Punctuality was Zoe's best if only attribute. Lina's stomach gurgled. She tore open the party picks, removed one and speared an olive. Eyeing the wine, she decided to be gracious and wait for Zoe.

Lunch had consisted of a salad sandwich. Trying to lose weight was hard, if not impossible. Lina had gone from a size twelve to a size sixteen in less than two years. Zoe was quite the opposite. She could get into size tens. Lina helped herself to some cheese.

It was a quarter to seven. Zoe had never been late before.

This night was her highlight of the week. She didn't have anything else to look forward to.

The phone rang. That would be Zoe now. Lina hurried to answer it.

'Hi, long time no talk.' It was Karla, her ex-flatmate.

'Oh, hello, Karla, what a surprise.' She hadn't rung for ages.

'How are you?' Lina asked.

'Down in the dumps, Derek's ditched me. He wouldn't give me a reason, just said it was over. I feel like crying on somebody's shoulder.'

'Well, make it mine. Come over. I could do with the company. It's just that I'm expecting Zoe. It's not like her to miss a wine and cheese night. She's nearly twenty minutes late.'

'Maybe she's got herself a bloke at last.' Said Karla.

'What! You must be kidding. The only man Zoe ever gets to see is the bloody priest at Mass and he's ancient.'

'How do you know? He could be a real spunk.'

'Look, I know her. Zoe tells me everything. She goes to Mass every Sunday. Never misses. She's a good Catholic girl.'

'Oh yeah, and pigs can fly. Did you two have an argument?'

'No, except for the usual squabbles. Zoe's forever moaning about something. But that wouldn't stop her from coming.'

'Maybe she needed some space,' Karla said.

Lina wasn't convinced.

'So I'll call around later. Got no man to keep me warm now.'

'Yeah, why not. See you soon.'

Lina decided not to ring Zoe, in case her mother answered. Where was she, though? Surely she just wouldn't disappear and not tell me. We've been friends for years.

The phone rang again. This had to be her.

It was Mrs Stoliski, Zoe's mother. 'Zoe never came home from work. Is she with you?' she shouted in her strong Polish accent. There was no greeting. Lina didn't expect one.

'No, Mrs Stoliski, she's not with me. I'm actually waiting for her. She's late.'

'Late! But I thought she had to be with you. All her clothes and things have gone.'

'What!' Lina gripped the receiver.

'So, she's not there.'

'No, I told you Mrs Stoliski. I don't know where she is. Wish I did. I'm sorry.'

'But where could she be? Do you know if she was seeing somebody?'

'Not unless it was the priest.' murmured Lina.

'What was that?'

'Nothing. I'll let you know if she arrives.'

'You do that!' barked Mrs Stoliski, then hung up.

Maybe Zoe was seeing someone. But if that was true, why didn't she tell me? I'm her best and only friend. Was it a sudden decision? Or had Zoe been planning to flee weeks, months ago?

Lina wandered into the kitchen. She opened the wine, poured a glass, then returned to the lounge to wait for Karla's arrival. She suddenly noticed an envelope lying on the carpet. How odd. It must have been slipped beneath the door while she was in the kitchen. Lina ripped it open.

Lina,
    Derek and I have left Sydney. Destination unknown. Thought it best this way. Tell Mum not to worry.
    Zoe.

The Other Half

'Two's company.' How often had I heard those words. Simplistic, yet sinister. At the time, I'd allowed naivety to rule. Loyalty, trust, where had that got me? What a fool I'd been. There were the warning signs, but I chose to ignore them: couldn't or didn't want to believe that Terry, Anna and Len had all been so devious. Playing games was their forte. Scruples? They had none.

Sinking into my armchair, I opened the photo album. Terry, fair-haired, green-eyed, with a great physique. 'Where did you find such a gorgeous bloke,' people would comment. I was the envy of everyone. We had met at a singles dinner and to my amazement, he showed interest in ordinary me.

There were angry shouts coming from next door's unit

After a few dates, Terry and I slept together. I wanted him to move in with me, but he was hesitant. 'Maybe later. Don't want to rush things, and anyway you'll wear me out.'

I had to admit I was in a state of euphoria, he was the most wonderful man I'd ever met. And I couldn't keep my hands off him.

A few weeks into our relationship, I arranged a meeting with my best friend Anna and her partner Len. Their relationship was an odd one. Even though they'd been together a long time, they never seemed to show any affection towards each other. Unlike Terry and I, who were often kissing, cuddling and whispering endearments.

Next door's shouting had stopped.

Anna and Len each had their own places, and they even went on separate holidays. She was forever complaining about his being so unreliable, and tight-fisted.

'Why do you put up with it, then?' I was scornful. 'Doesn't sound as if he makes you very happy.'

'Oh,' she'd reply, 'you wouldn't understand. Sometimes it's a case of better the devil you know.'

I studied a photo of Anna and Terry. She had an arm around his waist. Len stood in the background, grinning. It had been taken when we were at the beach one day. I shut my eyes. Terry lay face down on his towel, as Anna wearing a brief bikini squeezed drops of water from her long hair onto his back. He jumped and caught her by the ankle. She giggled.

'Len, darling, I want some suntan lotion rubbed on my back.'

He continued to toss the salad, 'Let Terry do it.' Len glanced at me, 'It's all right, isn't it?'

I nodded, 'Of course,' noticing how eager Anna was to untie her bikini top and fling herself down onto the towel.

Terry knelt beside her and rubbed in the lotion. I couldn't tell if he was enjoying it or not. Len lit a cigarette. I felt him watching me. Was my jealousy so obvious?

There was more noise from next door.

On Saturday nights, we'd drifted into the habit of going to Len's place for dinner. I wasn't too keen on the idea, but I had to concede that he was an excellent cook. After the meal, Terry and Len would discuss topics that neither Anna nor myself had the slightest interest in. If it wasn't computers, it was politics. She would go for a long bubble bath, while I'd feign attention in their conversation, by nodding in what I thought were the right places.

My holidays were due soon. I suggested that we visit my parents and brother in Adelaide. I wanted Terry to become part of my family, wanted us to get married, have children. I'd never told him about my brother being gay. Nobody knew, not even Anna.

My biggest regret was taking a day off work and calling on Terry unexpectedly. I'd planned to show him the brochures on Adelaide.

Len, barefoot, with ruffled hair and wearing a bathrobe, answered the door. What the hell was he doing here?

I was about to speak, when Terry called, 'Who is it?'

Len put a finger up to his lips. My tongue turned to cement. He reached out his hand. I recoiled. He shut the door. I managed to stumble down the steps and out into the street. Terry and Len in bed together? My stomach churned. How long had it been going on? Did Anna know? I bet she did. Terry, my lover, friend, confidant, a bisexual? I couldn't believe it. My legs trembled. Soon after, I retched into the gutter.

I did take my holidays, but didn't go to Adelaide. The only time I ventured from my flat was to buy the necessities and pay the rent.

Terry didn't contact me again and Anna had also vanished. Some friend. Her neighbour told me that she'd gone overseas. Len actually had the gall to ring me once, but as soon as I heard his voice, I hung up. The following day, I applied for a private number.

Friends. I banged shut the album. How could I ever trust anyone again?

An abrupt knock at the door startled me.

'Who is it?' I snapped.

'Sweetie…'

I cringed, It was the guy from next door.

'Could you be a darling and lend me your hairdryer. My other half won't lend me his.'

Let's Do Lunch

Another predictable lunch with my old school chum. There was some banter with the clean-shaven waiter as we studied the menus. I decided to have the vegetarian risotto, while she chose the entrée and a spaghetti marinara.

'Señora, would you like some wine?' the waiter asked my friend as he straightened the red checked tablecloth.

A heady smell of garlic permeated the air.

'Señora?' she repeated. 'It's signorina not señora.'

The waiter blushed and cleared his throat. 'Sorry, so sorry, signorina.' He looked at me.

I made no comment.

'I'll have a glass of Riesling,' she said, positioning the serviette onto her lap.

He turned to me. 'And you, miss?' He must have observed my ring-free fingers.

'No wine for me, thanks. I'll have a bottle of water.'

The waiter then whisked up the menus and made his exit.

'Gee,' she murmured, leaning across the table, 'I must be looking my age.'

Before I could reply, someone gave an uproarious shout. Corks popped and glasses clinked.

'Somebody's having a good time.' I said as the water, wine and her entrée arrived.

Diced zucchini, mushrooms and two slices of salami. She offered me some. I shook my head.

While she ate, we chatted about work, our acquaintances and my boyfriend, whom she disliked for some obscure reason. It had been five years since her last relationship.

'I've forgotten what it's like,' she tittered. 'I'm so out of practice.'

The woman seated at the table nearest us had orange hair and a ring through her nose. Her partner was bald and had an eyepatch. Various badges and safety pins adorned his corduroy jacket.

'Heard from your brother lately?' I asked.

'No, he hardly ever rings now, too busy with her family.' By her, she meant his de facto partner. 'And I rarely get to see my little niece. She'll be walking soon. They haven't even sent me any photos of her.'

Family squabbles bored me. I'd enough of my own. I decided to change the topic quickly. 'How's the rooster?' The rooster was her next-door neighbour's pet.

'Oh, him!' She pulled a face. 'He hasn't crowed for ages.'

'He could be dead.' I said.

'Yeah, he could be.' She moved her plate aside and licked each finger.

Our mains arrived. Mine looked and smelt delicious.

'We'll have to come again,' I said between mouthfuls of rice.

She nodded, dripping sauce onto her blouse. 'Lucky for me it's red.' She gave a hiccup, then signalled the waiter.

'Yes, signorina. What can I do for you?'

She grinned. 'Another glass of Riesling.'

'Certainly,' he replied.

Orange hair and Eyepatch were onto their second bottle of wine.

'We had this woman come to our door the other day trying to sell us a water filter. I've never met anyone so rude and she used scare tactics too.'

'How do you mean?'

'Well,' she said, shovelling in more spaghetti, 'she told us that our water was so contaminated that in a few years' time Dad and I could get anything from arthritis to dementia.'

'That's a bit extreme, isn't it?' I took a sip of water, and wondered whether it had been filtered.

The waiter, who was hovering close by, muttered something beneath his breath.

'I told this woman that I'd have to discuss it with Dad first and she had the hide to say, "I'll give you five minutes." She dressed like a tart with a low-cut top showing all her boobs and she wore a really short skirt. You should've seen my dad ogling her. Made me sick. I wanted to throw her out but he insisted she stay for a coffee.'

The waiter gave us an odd look.

'So how is your dad?' I asked.

'Oh, he's driving me crazy as usual. He's still after a woman and now he wants to go disco dancing of all things.' She snorted.

I found it hard to imagine her dad on the dance floor, dodging the flashing lights and the gyrating bodies.

We finished our meals. The waiter returned to the table, thrust the dessert menus at us then quickly collected our plates. I ordered a cappuccino and she a slice of cheesecake.

'What's eating him?' she said in a nonchalant tone.

'No idea,' I shrugged.

The dessert and coffee arrived. She devoured her cheesecake. I spooned half a teaspoon of sugar into my coffee and stirred it. I eyed the disappearing cheesecake, but resisted the temptation to order any.

Suddenly, she gave a loud gasp.

'What's up?'

'I just saw Dad walk in.'

'So?' I frowned.

'He's with that woman.' She snatched a menu from the table beside us and hid behind it.

'What woman?'

'The one who tried to con us into buying that water filter. They haven't seen me yet, but I think we'd better get going.' She caught the waiter's attention. 'Can we have the bill?' she whispered.

'Certainly,' he gave a brief nod, 'but if you'll excuse me, that woman you referred to earlier is my sister and I can assure you that she is not a con, nor is she a tart.'

Her face went red. She stammered, 'I'm sorry, I cidn't…'

I had to suppress a giggle.

'Now, signorina, or was that señora,' he said, giving a wave to his sister, 'are you sure you won't have another of our lovely desserts?'

Wasp and Whistle

I finally arrive in Windrush Village, England, after years of corresponding with Aunt Elsie. Arrive to rows of terraces, cul-de-sacs and the flutter of curtains. Isn't that the niece from Australia? I could imagine the whispers. My aunt being very chatty, has probably told her neighbours all about me, from my job as a legal secretary to my recent divorce.

The village, with its sandstone cottages and cobblestone paths, has a greengrocer, post office, two churches and a Tudor-style inn, the Wasp and Whistle. The publican, a Mr Nash, reminds me of a Charles Dickens character with his long ginger sideburns and his striped waistcoat. Another incident amuses me and that is watching letters slip through the vent in the front door. The invisible postman. How very civilised not to have one's mailbox outside, especially when it's cold and wet.

Aunt Elsie can't wait until I step indoors before she starts with her chatter. 'Man mad, she is.'

'Who?' I ask, shrugging off my coat and hanging it on a hook in the hallway.

'Roly Poly.'

'Oh her,' I grin. 'So who is the lucky man this time?' I give my hair a quick comb.

Aunt Elsie eases herself into an armchair, clasps her mottled hands and begins to tell me about Roly Poly, who is now after the plumber.

'He's much too young for her, but he must like them big.' She gives a loud tut. 'She's the talk of the whole village. Should be ashamed of herself!'

Mrs Peck, Aunt Elsie's cleaner, must have been in today. On the mantelpiece, I notice a shepherd boy back to front and a small penguin on its back.

'That Mrs Gibble round the corner is forever trying to get Mrs Peck to move her wardrobes. She's even said she'd pay her more,' said Aunt Elsie. 'She even used to iron her knickers. No wonder Tom ran off with that brassy barmaid and her nearly twenty years younger.' Aunt Elsie stands and heads towards the kitchen.

I met Mrs Gibble recently, a thin woman with bleached hair and a lizard tongue. I resent her probing questions, such as the purpose of my visit and how long did I plan to stay.

'That Mrs Gibble is a real stickybeak,' I say as my aunt returns to the lounge with bowls of ham and pea soup.

'Stickybeak? What's that, dear?' she asks, lifting her spoon.

'It's a person too fond of wanting to know all your business.'

'Oh, we call that sort here nosey parkers.' She gives a sniff.

What I could not get used to was the total lack of privacy. The upstairs rooms give me complete viewing access into the next-door neighbour's back gardens. I always feel so conspicuous, in case anyone glances up and spots me. Also the bathrooms are all upstairs. Aunt Elsie has no shower and looks bewildered when I ask why.

'Nobody messes with showers, dear, it's the weekly bath, or a wash in the sink. The trouble with you Australians is that you wash too much, take all the natural oils out of your skin.'

Sunday lunch is a staunch tradition. We either have roast beef or lamb. Mad cow disease, she claims, is a plot invented by new age extremists to scare people from eating meat and force them into becoming vegetarians.

'Carrots and salad is rabbit food,' she utters if I ever refuse any of the beef or lamb. 'Your Uncle Lou lived to be ninety and he ate meat everyday and had his few whiskies too. But he never went to the Wasp and Whistle of a weekend.'

'Why was that?'

'Too many young ones in there and those bands with their wretched music drove him insane. You should go along one night, dear. Better than sitting in with an old woman like me.'

'No, Aunt Elsie, that's not my scene. I stopped going to live bands years ago. Anyway, I'd sooner listen to you reminiscing.'

She sinks into her armchair. 'We wore hats back then. High heels and lots of make-up. Young women now don't know how to dress.'

I couldn't imagine my aunt in high heels, never mind make-up.

'How did you and Uncle Lou meet?'

'Oh, your Uncle Lou and me were a blind date.'

I gape. 'Really?'

'Yes, well, it was arranged by a cousin of mine. The family was worried that I'd be left on the shelf.'

'I'll bet it was much easier to meet someone decent back then,' I say, thinking about some of the losers I'd met over the years.

'Well, I wouldn't say that, dear. You still got your drinkers, your wife-beaters and your spongers. I guess I was just lucky with your uncle.' She stands, draws the curtains, then switches on the light. 'The nuns, Sister Ruth and Sister Judith, are popping in tomorrow.'

Aunt Elsie looks forward to their weekly visits and makes sure that she always has her best tablecloth and china ready. Despite her chirpy front, she is very lonely. I tried to interest her in the church hall's activities, but she refuses to go because all the members are in cliques and all they ever talk about is their grandchildren. Aunt Elsie never had a family of her own.

'The sisters could do with a hand at their jumble sale tomorrow,' she hints, bending to turn on the gas heater.

I shiver. There is an unmistakable rawness in the air.

'I'd die here in winter.'

'No you wouldn't, dear, you'd just put on extra clothes.'

A sudden knock at the door startles us.

'Now who could that be?' Aunt Elsie bustles out of the lounge and into the hall.

Moments later, Roly Poly enters the room. She nods to me. Her eyeshadow is thick and her lipstick is too gaudy. 'I've just come for the papers.'

I give her a blank look.

'She means all my old newspapers, they only clutter up the place.'

Roly Poly plonks herself on the arm of the sofa. There is a ladder in her stocking. 'I come to your aunt's for the newspapers and to Mrs Gibble for the magazines.'

'Would you like some tea?' asks Aunt Elsie as she hands Roly Poly a bundle of papers.

'Oh, no ta. Got bingo tonight. Must get home and sharpen me pencils.'

After she goes, I ask my aunt, 'Why can't she buy her own newspapers and magazines?'

Aunt Elsie tells me that Roly Poly wouldn't spend a quid unless she had to. 'She grabs loads of paper towels from public toilets and she's even charged me for petrol.'

'What!'

'Yes, first and last time. We went to see a friend of hers who lives on a farm. She even promised me a jar or two of jam and I'm still waiting! Bingo, huh! Who is she kidding? She's too busy chasing that young plumber. Don't they call them toy boys now?'

I yawn. 'Yeah, they do.' I glance at the clock, almost nine and still light. 'Think I'll turn in, there isn't much on the tele.' I kiss my aunt on the cheek before heading upstairs.

I am about to about to pull down the doona when I hear raised voices and a car door slam. I quickly go to the window.

'You old trollop! I'm warning you. Stay away from my man.'

Who is that? I take a peep, then gasp. Shaking a fist at Roly Poly is the publican, Mr Nash. Close by, leaning against his van, is the young plumber. Roly Poly wobbles in her high heels as she clutches a bottle of wine. I'll bet it's a cheap brand, I muse. Hell's bells. I wonder if Aunt Elsie has heard all the commotion. Stifling a giggle, I flee downstairs.

Valentino

Anna yanks the doona around her ears. She rubs her numb feet against one another, then shoves aside the cold water bottle. This morning she has an appointment for a facial and leg waxing. Afternoons are for lazing on the sofa and reading erotic fiction. She wishes that next door's terrier would shut up. *I should've poisoned the bloody thing years ago.* Anna is not ashamed of her thoughts. She doesn't like dogs. They are too loyal, too loving.

She examines the cracks in the wall. Cracks like the fragmentary relationship between Anna and her mother. Dreams of a stout woman with small eyes and two hairs sprouting from her chin continue to persecute Anna. Closing her eyes, she could still hear her mother's taunts and threats to be home before midnight. But the taunts and the threats soon diminished as the cancer ferociously spread. On the day of the funeral, Anna wore three-inch stilettos, a short skirt and red lipstick. She didn't cry. Her father, looking crumpled, muttered to himself during the eulogy.

'Anna, take that lipstick off at once!' her moustached aunt had snapped. She'd thrust a tissue at her. 'You're a disgrace to your family, coming to your mamma's funeral dressed like a whore!'

Anna had ignored her and the proffered tissue. Relatives whom she hadn't seen in years huddled like whispering vultures. One spoke in a loud voice, 'She's a wicked girl, sent her poor mamma to an early grave.'

She sidled up to them, pulled out her compact mirror and applied more lipstick. Anna enjoyed seeing their looks of horror. Relatives. Weddings and funerals were the only times when they'd bother to make an appearance.

Not one of them came near the house when her mother was ill. After the funeral, her uncle had the audacity to approach her with, 'You're nearly thirty. You should be thinking about settling down. I know a nice boy.'

But Anna didn't want a nice boy. They were too predictable. She preferred the thrill of one-night stands.

Soon after her mother's death, Anna persuaded her father to enter an aged care hostel. She did not intend playing nursemaid.

He had his own room and was free to come and go. What he did complain about was the food: it was either undercooked or overcooked. The sauce was too watery and they never used salt. He'd been spoilt by her mother.

'Salt's no good for you, papa, with your heart condition. You know that.' Anna grew bored having to repeat the same advice.

They would meet once a fortnight.

On the last occasion, he told Anna bluntly, 'I need a woman. I can't live on my own.'

She was stunned, disgusted even. 'A woman at your age, papa, but mamma's only been gone six months. You're nearly sixty-five. Don't be so ridiculous.' She gave an embarrassed laugh, hoping that nobody in the café had heard them.

'I've been doing some internet dating.'

'What! I don't believe I'm hearing this. You know too much excitement's no good for your heart. Remember what the doctor said.' That would scare him. The old fool. A woman at his age. The very idea was repulsive.

A month after his disclosure he rang Anna to tell her that he'd met someone. 'She's a really nice lady, Anna. I want you to meet her. I've told her all about you.'

'Oh, have you now. Well, I'm not interested in meeting her. Got that?' She hung up.

The woman is after his house. Can't he see that. He is so gullible. Such a child in many ways. What does this woman see in him anyway?

It couldn't be for his looks: receding hair and a pot belly. Think's he's Valentino all of a sudden.

When her father died, the house would be hers. No bitch was going to get her hands on it.

An unexpected knock at the door startled her. It wasn't even eight o'clock. Who could be visiting so early? Anna opened the door. Standing on the step was her father in a smart cream jacket and navy tie. Next to him was an attractive woman in her fifties, holding a suitcase.

'Good morning, Anna.' Her father smiled. 'I'd like you to meet Isobel. We got married yesterday.'

Not George

The park again. The same park. Christmas Day, The Greek Easter even, Martina doesn't care. She is eager to escape the whispering mice that nibble on food scraps beneath her bed. Eating mouldy sandwiches, or singing nursery rhymes to herself in the park, Martina is oblivious to the weather, or the stares from onlookers. There is no sign of the bag lady yet, pleasantries are exchanged, but never names or confidences. Whenever the bag lady leaves, she always tugs on her earring before pushing her loaded trolley down the path.

A girl in a frilly dress skips past. She reminds Martina of her daughter Vicky when she was a child. Life was so simple when her husband was alive and the children were small. Martina's son George lives with her. He isn't much company, but lately he's become sullen, withdrawn. He often goes out and doesn't return until the early hours of the morning. He never tells her where he goes or what he does and he'd recently got into the habit of scribbling hate messages on the walls. His appearance and hygiene is deteriorating too, with hair halfway down his back and not a shower in weeks. If he could find a job, and make friends, things would be so much better. George is a good boy, even if he does get angry at times.

One afternoon, Martina ventures into his room. The window is shut and smelly clothes are strewn across the floor. Her husband only had to punch George for him to obey. There was a time when her son came home with stains on his shirt cuffs and a scratch on his cheek.

Martina had mentioned this episode to Vicky, but her reaction had been, 'I don't care about George. He was always weird.'

'But Vicky, he's your brother,' Martina had spluttered.

'Brother! You call him a normal person. Don't make me laugh, Mother! I'm ashamed of him, and you.'

For seven days a week, Martina and her husband had worked in their milk bar, paid for Vicky's private school fees and a lavish wedding which ended in divorce shortly after.

Martina watches as a young man with long hair and scruffy jeans throws a ball for his dog. Her thoughts return to her son. Last week, her neighbour revealed that she'd seen George in the city one night. He'd been darting in and out of traffic and abusing drivers. Martina didn't believe her. It can't have been George. It has to have been somebody else. Somebody who looked like him. He wouldn't do anything so stupid.

Martina scans the park. The bag lady isn't coming. Maybe she's found another bench, another soul to chat with. Martina pulls at her black-fringed shawl and makes her way home. The house is silent. Is George still out?

She looks in his room to make sure. Inside the kitchen, she switches on the radio. 'An elderly woman was found strangled early today in Brampton Park.' She turns up the volume. 'A man who was last seen in the vicinity of the area is wanted for questioning by police. He is Caucasian, in his thirties, with long dark hair, between one hundred and seventy centimetres and one hundred and eighty centimetres tall.'

A wail escapes Martina's lips as she notices a woman's earring on the table. It looks exactly like the one that the bag lady used to wear. But how did it get here? Did George find it? Had he been in the park? Did he know the bag lady?

The front door slams shut. Martina jumps. Footsteps thud along the corridor. She grips the edge of the table, eyes the knife in the drainer, then slowly turns.

Something Sinister

Leonie was odd, thought Ruby as she waited outside the Ink Spot gift store at The Rocks. She'd never felt comfortable in Leonie's company. They had little in common and at times Ruby wondered why she even bothered.

It was almost five o'clock. Leonie should be here soon. She was punctual if nothing else. A few ice cream lickers sauntered past. Ruby tucked a strand of hair behind her ear. A bite to eat, a tour of The Rocks, then a movie, might not be such a bad idea, better than being cooped up inside her stuffy bedsitter.

There was a tap on her shoulder. 'Hi.' Leonie ran a hand through her short mousey hair. 'Been waiting long?' Before Ruby could reply, Leonie went on, 'They should be here soon.'

'Who?'

'Oh, didn't I tell you? I've invited two friends along. Knew you wouldn't mind. They're from my social group, Cool Connections.'

Ruby refrained from saying that in fact she did mind.

Leonie handed her a crumpled piece of paper. 'This is their latest newsletter.'

'Thanks.' She shoved it into her bag. 'I'll read it later.'

'I told them what time we'd be meeting.' Leonie looked up and down the street. She picked at a pimple on her chin. It bled. 'Hell!' She dabbed it with a tissue.

Ruby noticed the rapid approach of two men. One of them waved.

'Thought you weren't coming.' Leonie threw away the tissue.

The older of the men wore a brown- spotted waistcoat and matching trousers. He had sparse grey hair and a goatee beard. Glasses hung from

a cord around his neck. He pecked Leonie on the cheek, then nodded
to Ruby. He introduced himself as Jasper. The other man with a pock-
marked complexion wore jeans and sandals. He made no attempt to
introduce himself.

'This is Darius,' said Jasper, putting on his glasses.

Leonie turned to Ruby. 'Jasper owns a bookshop specialising in first
editions.'

'Oh, how interesting.' she replied without any real enthusiasm.

'You're not a reader, I take it?' Jasper peered at her, stroking his
goatee.

'Well, I…'

'Never mind.'

They made a move. Leonie and Jasper walked on ahead.

Darius sidled up to Ruby. 'Did Leonie tell you much about our social group?'

'No, but she did give me one of the newsletters. I haven't read it
yet.'

'You could say that our outings differ a little to your average group.'

Ruby was about to ask in what way, when Jasper spun round. 'We
need to eat. How about some light refreshments at our usual café, then
we'll go on a tour of The Rocks and later a film. That suit you, Ruby?'

'Yes, fine by me.'

'You are easy to please,' whispered Darius.

'You were going to tell me about your group outings,' she reminded
him.

'We've got midnight cemetery walks, ghost hunts and visits to a few
naughty burlesque shows. How's that for a start?' He gave her a furtive
look.

Ruby shivered, then rubbed her arms. Perhaps it was all a joke. They
seemed harmless enough, a bit eccentric maybe. Funny how Leonie had
never told her about these strange outings. What had she got herself
into?

'How did you and Leonie meet?' he asked.

'Through an ex flatmate.'

'That brother of hers was a bit of a troublemaker. He was a member of our group, until he vanished.'

'Brother? I never knew she had a brother.'

'Yeah, didn't Leonie tell you? He went missing months ago.'

Ruby was stunned. Why didn't Leonie tell her she had a brother? What was the big secret?

They entered the café and placed their orders. She wasn't feeling very hungry.

'Leonie,' said Jasper biting into his Danish pastry, 'have you booked Blim Cottage yet?'

'No. I haven't.'

'Why ever not?' He thumped the table.

Ruby jumped.

'What's got into you, woman!'

Leonie spluttered on her glass of cordial. 'Well, Jasper, I don't feel all that comfortable returning to Blim Cottage, not after my brother disappeared. I'm sorry.'

Jasper ferreted crumbs from his goatee. 'You're sorry!' He glared at her.

'What cottage is this?' Ruby couldn't contain her curiosity any longer. Leonie had never told her about a cottage.

Darius leaned forward, 'It's our hideaway in the mountains. Fantastic for those night prowls.' He touched her hand and winked at her.

She flinched. Pushed her toast aside. 'How many of you go to this cottage?'

'Just us three, but a foursome would be ideal. Want to come?' Darius studied his manicured fingernails.

Jasper sniggered. 'Darius, dear fellow, she just can't come to Blim Cottage. She has to become a member of our group first. Agree to the rules and it's me who decides if she's suitable or not. It takes a special kind of person.'

'Special in what way?' Ruby swallowed. Her tongue felt like a scouring pad.

Leonie was tearing her serviette into tiny pieces.

Darius looked at Jasper. 'Can I tell her?'

Jasper hesitated for a moment or so, then nodded.

'It's like this,' Darius ran a finger along the blade of his knife. He lowered his voice, 'We like to create our own kind of chaos, we assume other identities. I'll be the hangman, while Jasper here plays the grave-digger. Leonie plays our victim. We all smoke a joint first, just to spice things up.'

Ruby felt queasy. Wanted to escape.

'That's quite enough, Darius,' hissed Jasper.

'What about that time I handcuffed you…'

'Enough, I said.' Jasper thumped the table again.

This was no joke. These people were serious.

'Now, Ruby, you realise why I must insist on the person's suitability. But since you're a friend of Leonie's…' He signalled for the bill.

Just how involved was Leonie? Ruby was confused. And how much did she know about her brother's disappearance? Had he participated in these bizarre rituals?

They left the café. Jasper gave his glasses a savage wipe.

Ruby wanted to run. Run back to her stuffy safe bedsitter and never have to see these people again.

Darius placed an arm around Leonie. She shrugged him off.

'It's been a pleasure, dear.' Jasper gave Ruby his card.

'No, thanks.'

'Keep it, I insist.' He thrust it into her hand. 'You may change your mind.'

Leonie avoided her gaze. She picked at another pimple.

Darius scratched his nether region.

What a sleaze, thought Ruby. After a quick goodbye, she turned on her heel. The disappearance of Leonie's brother kept nagging at her. Had he been blackmailing all three? Why hadn't Leonie ever mentioned him? None of them, especially Jasper, respectable bookshop owner, would like anyone to discover their macabre games.

She threw his number into the bin. Moments later, her mobile signalled a text: *Be careful. We're watching you.*

Nailing It

Lionel was a scrounger. And nothing but. I only tolerated him because he was my partner's mate. They'd met at lawn bowls ten years ago and were now best mates. Lionel suffered from emphysema, although it didn't stop him from flirting with other women, despite his relationship with Ellie. Apparently, Ellie's previous marriage had been chaos. Her ex-husband was abusive, and a heavy drinker. Lionel was quite the opposite. He never swore in front of women and was always the first to open a door. Whenever Lionel stayed at Paul's place, he would get all of his washing and cooking done, and Paul would even cut Lionel's toenails.

Curious, I asked my partner once, 'Why do you cut his toenails?'

'Because Lionel has trouble bending to even tie his shoelaces. He gets out of breath very easily. You know how bad his emphysema is.'

Not bad enough for him to abstain from playing his bowls and spending time in smoky clubs, I wanted to spout.

After three months of living together, Lionel and Ellie no longer shared a bed. Lionel made the excuse, 'Ellie likes the window open all night, the cold air would kill me, that's why we sleep separately.'

Her story was, 'Lionel got upset with me when he found my Bibles and religious tapes hidden at the back of the wardrobe. He filled the bathtub and drowned them. That's when I decided on separate sleeping arrangements. I even lock my bedroom door and refuse to do his cooking or his washing.'

I was puzzled as to what they had in common. Lionel's only other interest outside of bowls was having a few bets on the horses. Ellie loathed gambling. She coordinated a Bible study group and went to church every Sunday.

Paul didn't like her. 'She's a liar, said she was giving up that crazy religion once she moved in with Lionel. Told me that she'd thrown out all her Bibles and stuff, then he goes and finds them hidden. And another strange thing is she asked me how long did I think Lionel had to live. I mean, what kind of a question is that?

Yes, I had to admit it was very strange. If Ellie was after his money, she'd be in for a big shock. He only had his disability pension, unlike her ex, who was very well-off.

'No wonder Lionel drowned all her books and crap. He should've bloody drowned her!' Paul scowled.

'Maybe she's afraid of him, that's why she locks her door,' I said.

'What, Lionel! Are you kidding? He wouldn't hurt a fly.'

That conversation took place a week ago.

Lionel entered the kitchen and sat at the table. His sparse ginger hair was uncombed and his small eyes were sleep encrusted. He'd arrived yesterday, armed with his dirty washing and his overgrown toenails.

'She's disappeared,' he said.

'Who?' I asked.

Paul turned away from frying his bacon and eggs, 'Yeah, who, mate?'

'Ellie.' He poured himself a cup of tea, 'Been gone for three days, no sign of her, even when I left to come here.'

'Maybe she's staying with a friend.' I took a sip of coffee.

'No, I tried them all. Even that church mob reckons they haven't seen her. Funny thing is, my mower and my walking stick have gone too.'

'I bet she's sold them on you.' Paul always ready to crucify her.

'What would she want with them? I reckon some kids pinched the mower, sold it for drug money, but who'd want my walking stick?' He yawned, the buttons on his pyjama jacket strained. He patted his copious stomach. 'Smells good, mate.'

Paul placed the breakfast in front of Lionel.

'But surely Ellie's not in the habit of just going off,' I insisted, trying to keep the annoyance out of my voice.

Paul emptied cornflakes into his bowl. Lionel salted his eggs.

I buttered my toast. 'Aren't you even wondering where Ellie is?' I glared at him.

'Ellie couldn't cook, you know. She even used to burn my chops.' He chuckled.

'Huh! Typical,' mumbled Paul.

'Bugger your chops! You're speaking about your partner as though she were dead.' I wanted to wring his neck.

Paul tapped me on the arm. 'Love, don't keep at it. Can't you see that Lionel is upset enough?'

I sighed and finished my toast.

Lionel dipped his bread into the egg and bacon fat. 'That was scrumptious, mate.' He belched loudly.

'I see that you haven't lost your appetite.' I felt like a pot about to boil over.

Lionel, ignoring, me said, 'I'm going to watch the cricket, mate.' He stood and made his exit from the kitchen.

Paul began to clear the table, 'Will you stop nagging him,' he hissed.

'Nagging him! His partner is missing, and he's making no effort to find her.'

Paul turned on the taps, adding dishwashing liquid into the sink. I grabbed a tea towel, leaned against the stove and thought about the reasons why I stayed with Paul. He was kind, a great cook and forever eager to wash up. Domesticity, he revelled in it. Our arguments, whenever we had any, were usually about Lionel.

'Did you know that they were thinking of splitting up?' Paul asked.

'Now, why does that not surprise me? I don't know why they got together in the first place.'

'Ellie wanted to, not Lionel. Her Bibles weren't enough to keep her warm at night. And he of course thought she'd take care of him.' He rinsed the knives and forks. 'Don't be such a drama queen,' Paul came over and tweaked my cheek. 'She'll turn up, don't worry. Look, if it makes you feel any better, I'll persuade him to call the police. Okay?'

There was no need to, as the police rang us a moment or two later. They wanted to speak to Lionel.

He entered the kitchen slowly, very slowly, and he was coughing. He'd had ample time to rehearse.

I hovered, but Paul pulled me into our bedroom and shut the door.

'You think he's done something don't you?' He gripped my arm.

'Done what?' I pulled away.

'You think he…'

There was a tap on the door.

'She's turned up, mate.' Lionel said.

We opened the door to find him standing there, an egg smear on his chin.

'She just walked into a cop station and gave herself up. Told them that she'd killed her husband, bashed him with my walking stick and put on the mower so nobody would hear his screams. They'd never got divorced. Maybe she was after his money.'

'Bloody hell!' Paul gave a low whistle. 'What a calculating bitch.' His face was white.

I suddenly felt shivery, had to sit down.

Paul put a hand on Lionel's shoulder. 'You know, you've always got my support whatever happens, mate. You can stay here as long as you like.'

'Yeah, thanks, Paul. I've gotta go to the station now, cops want to ask me some questions. I'd better get ready.'

He was making his way towards the spare room, when I said, 'I expect the police will want to know where you were on the day Ellie's husband was murdered.' I was amazed at how steady my voice sounded. 'I mean, there could have been an accomplice.'

Lionel turned to Paul. 'I was here all the time, wasn't I, mate?'

'Yeah, sure you were.' Paul cleared his throat. 'Wasn't he, darling?'

They both looked at me.

The Vestal Virgin

'You don't mind if Melita comes, do you?' asked Jaylene on the phone in between chewing. She was forever eating; no wonder she was so obese.

I paused for a moment. Did I really want to see Melita? We had gone to the same secondary school. She knew me when I wore braces and I knew her when she was anorexic. It must be close to twenty years since we'd last seen each other. She was always the loner at school, whereas I'd been the class chatterbox. We had never been close.

'No, I don't mind, the more the merrier.' I hoped I sounded convincing.

'Shall we meet at the usual place on Saturday then, say about midday?' Jaylene replied.

'Yes, why not?' The usual place being Carla's Coffee Shop inside our local plaza.

I lit another cigarette and made a vow to give up my ten-a-day habit. But we all had our weaknesses. Mine was smoking, Jaylene's was food. And Melita's… I expected we'd find out on Saturday.

When I arrived at the coffee shop, Jaylene was already gorging on a hamburger and chips. 'Couldn't wait.'

'So I see.' I sat down.

'Have one?' She indicated the bowl of chips.

'No, thanks.' I studied the menu, then placed my order with the pimply-faced waitress. I watched as the hamburger quickly vanished. 'Shouldn't we wait for Melita?'

'No, why should we? Anyway, I was starving. And guess what, they haven't done it yet, you know.'

'Who hasn't done what?'

'Here's Melita now. Tell you later.' Jaylene waved to a tall dark-haired woman who'd entered the café and drifted over to our table.

Melita was still very thin. She caught me staring. I looked away. My cheese on toast and milkshake had arrived.

'You could have waited for me.' Melita frowned.

'I thought you'd be late,' Jaylene said.

Melita ignored her and ordered a coffee.

'Is that all you're having?' Jaylene looked horrified.

'Yes. I'm not hungry.'

I bit into my toast. 'Long time no see, Melita. Seems like yesterday when we were at school, doesn't it?' Anything to lighten the mood.

She gave me a half-smile. School, with its neurotic teachers and boring lessons. Did Melita ever reminisce about those days?

'So, are you working, studying?' I asked, as though I was really interested.

'Working.' Her tone lacked enthusiasm.

'What do you do?'

'Data entry for an insurance company. It's only temporary, three months.'

I nodded.

'How's Gary?' asked Jaylene.

'Oh, he's fine, working tonight.' She turned to me. 'He works in a bakery, been made supervisor recently.'

'So you'd never be short of bread then,' I replied, being flippant.

She didn't respond. 'You know I still can't introduce him to my sister or her family.' Melita toyed with the band on her wristwatch.

'Why, for God's sake? You've known him long enough,' Jaylene snapped.

'Yeah, I know, but he still dresses like a dag. That's what embarrasses me.'

Jaylene raised her eyes. 'So what! He sounds like a nice guy. Wish I had someone like him.'

Melita sighed, brushing a hand through her hair.

'I'm dying for a smoke,' I said.

'Smoking's bad for you,' Jaylene said as she ordered a Danish pastry.

And so is stuffing your face, I felt like adding.

'If Gary dressed up a bit more, I'd introduce him to my sister but…' Melita gazed into her now empty cup.

'It's your life, not your bloody sister's. Why are you always trying to please her?' Jaylene scratched a blemish on her cheek.

'I know, but I'm still not sure if he's the one.'

'What do you mean?' I asked.

'Well, I really like him. He's my age, single, good-looking, but…' Melita leaned towards us and hissed, 'He wants us to have sex.'

'What's wrong with that? I'd be more worried if he didn't want to do it,' Jaylene tittered.

I stirred my milkshake.

'I'm Catholic, go to Mass regularly and I'm in a Bible study group,' said Melita.

'So?' I wished she'd get to the point.

'What I think Melita is trying to say is that she's a good Catholic girl and doesn't believe in sex before marriage. Am I right?' asked Jaylene.

Melita confirmed it. I drank the remainder of my milkshake.

'But from what you told me the other day, you and Gary have just done about everything else. You go to bed together, do foreplay but when it comes to penetration, you stop. You're only frustrating the guy. How long are you going to keep playing these stupid games?' Jaylene drummed her fingers on the table.

I was amazed. How could Melita be so naïve, immature?

'Well, at least I'm still a virgin, unlike you two.'

'Yeah, and I call myself a Born Again Virgin,' Jaylene grinned. 'You know, I haven't done it in five years, even forgotten what it's like now. How about you?' She turned to me. 'Any luck on the men front?'

I shook my head. My relationship had ended six months earlier and I hadn't bothered with anyone since.

'I go to reconciliation every week,' Melita piped up.

'What have you got to confess? I mean, you haven't even done it yet, unless you want to count the foreplay.' Jaylene gave a loud belch. 'Excuse me.'

'Look, I just want to be sure, that's all. And anyway, the Pope doesn't believe in sex before marriage. He doesn't even allow condoms.' She gave us a smug smile.

'What would he bloody know! He's nearly a hundred,' Jaylene said as she opened her pocket mirror and applied a plum lipstick.

This conversation was getting ridiculous, but I was determined to rattle Melita. 'What you're doing with Gary is a sin anyway.'

'What do you mean?' Her eyes widened.

'Well, it's just as big a sin to even get into bed with him.'

Jaylene agreed. 'She's right, if you really stood by your beliefs, you wouldn't even go that far.'

The next twenty minutes or so, we talked about fashions, make-up, and the latest reality show. Eventually we stood, then made our way to the counter.

Jaylene sidled up to Melita. 'I suggest you just do it.'

'Yeah, you don't want to die wondering, do you?' I found it hard to keep a straight face.

We split, promising to meet again in about a month's time.

A week later, Jaylene rang. 'You wouldn't believe what's happened.'

'What?'

'Melita's devastated.'

'Why? What's up?'

'Remember how she was talking about Gary and thinking about whether to do it?'

'Yeah, how could I forget?' I lit a cigarette, anxious to hear the rest.

'Well, she's just discovered that he wasn't single, he had a wife and kids in the country.'

'Hell! How did she find out?'

'The wife turned up on his doorstep with the kids. She hadn't heard from him in ages and she was behind with the rent and bills. Apparently, the bastard hadn't been sending her any money. Just before the wife arrived, Melita had told him she was willing to go all the way.'

In spite of the circumstances, I had to grin. Melita faced with a distraught wife and kids, as she was about to…

So nothing had changed. I still had my smokes, Jaylene her addiction to food, and Melita, well, she still had her prized virginity.

Prelude at Piccolo's

Jan gulped the rest of her third Bacardi and coke. She scanned Piccolo's Wine Bar. No potentials here yet. She didn't mind coming on her own, always met plenty of men and even got naughty with some.

She knew her weaknesses. Alcohol, a good-looking man and Jan was hooked. She shifted on the stool, swung her newly waxed legs and smoothed her hands over her miniskirt.

To celebrate her recent fortieth birthday, she had taken home two bottles of champagne and a twenty-three-year-old sales rep. No commitments, no emotional ties, that's the way Jan wanted it.

She snatched a handful of nuts.

Clarissa, an acquaintance, dressed in white jeans and a midriff top, entered Piccolo's. She drifted over to Jan. 'Hello. stranger, you're in early today.' She hopped onto the stool alongside.

'Yeah, managed to get a half flex day.'

Clarissa, with her perfect figure and shoulder-length hair, was a fitness addict and a regular at her local gym. Having outlived two prosperous husbands, the cow was now onto her third. How did she do it? Not that Jan was ever drawn to the idea of marriage, but the money would've been handy.

'What are you drinking?' Clarissa asked, applying a plum lipstick.

'Why? You shouting?' Jan was taken aback, she wasn't usually so generous.

'Yep. Gotta spend some of Marcus's money.'

Marcus, now there's a coincidence. Jan was intrigued. The guy she'd met at Piccolos's on a few occasions had introduced himself as Marcus.

Maybe he was Clarissa's husband? But did Jan really care? Husbands had never been part of her exclusion zone before.

'Are you okay?'

'Yes, fine,' grinned Jan. 'Just miles away. Well, seeing it's your shout, I'll have another Bacardi and Coke.'

She studied Clarissa as she ordered their drinks. Both husbands had died in obscure circumstances. Soon after the last one keeled over, Clarissa went on a cruise. Her way of coping with grief, loss, or was it a chance to meet husband number three?

Their drinks arrived. Clarissa toyed with her chunky bracelet.

Jan sucked on an ice cube. 'I've been seeing this real spunk in here.'

'And…?' Clarissa raised an eyebrow.

'He rang me late last night wanting me to meet him for dinner.'

'Did you go?'

'No, but can't say I wasn't tempted.'

Clarissa smirked. 'Bloody men. All got one thing on their minds.' Tossing back her drink, Clarissa said, 'I'd better go. Got an aerobics class soon. See you.' She pecked her on the cheek and left.

Jan's stomach rumbled. She felt light-headed. I should have eaten something earlier, she thought.

A hand brushed her shoulder. She turned. There stood Marcus in an open-neck shirt. His blond hair looked damp, as if he'd been for a swim or had had a shower.

Removing her glasses, Jan gave her eyes a frantic rub.

'Oh, I'm for real all right. May I?' He indicated the stool.

'Sure.'

He sat down. 'What are you drinking?' He pulled out his wallet.

Jan shook her head. 'Think I've had too many now.'

'Sorry, shouldn't have called you so late last night, got caught up with things. How about we go for that meal now?'

Jan couldn't believe her luck. 'I've got a better idea. How about we go back to my place? I've got plenty of food and bubbly.'

'Sounds good to me.' He ran a finger gently along her arm.

So what if he was Clarissa's man. She didn't deserve him anyway.

The Visit

May could not forget her cousin Nick's parting words. 'We're family. Got to keep in touch, especially now that I've found you after all these years.'

He was no more than twenty, twenty-one at the most, when he'd disappeared four decades ago.

She closed the door, then made her way through the hall and into the kitchen. The figurines on the Welsh dresser needed a good dust. She didn't have the energy or the enthusiasm any more. She refilled the sugar bowl, then began to clear the table. Visitors, she huffed; they made more work than enough. Pouring the tea dregs into the sink and running the tap slowly, May watched them escaping down the plughole.

Escaping, just like Nick had done. Why did he do it? Was it the fear of responsibility, the inevitable boredom of marriage, that made him want to abandon everybody? What a shock she'd got when he rang her this morning. She'd almost dropped the receiver.

May sat down and lit a cigarette. Aunt Jessie in England had given Nick her number. Apparently, he was there two months ago. She stood rubbing her tailbone. Wind rattled the window. She shuffled over to close it. Why did he suddenly decide to make himself known? It was puzzling. She stubbed out her cigarette. The worst part about his reappearance was his casual attitude. He showed no remorse.

May bit her lip. She hadn't been game to ask him any direct questions concerning his past. Why he'd deserted his wife when she was expecting their child. Even Aunt Jessie, who'd doted on him like a son, had no idea where he'd gone. He was a mystery, determined to keep everyone in the dark. May had assumed that he'd met with foul play.

His wife eventually remarried. Well, who could blame her? She wasn't going to sit around for forty years and wait for him to show up.

He's got a nerve, May fumed, turning up out of the blue, wanting to talk about old times as though it were yesterday. I should've been more outspoken and demanded some answers. He's not going to start snooping into my life. My yesterdays were buried a long time ago. We're strangers. I don't owe him a thing. May lit another cigarette.

She had to admit he'd hardly changed, still had that mop of ginger hair, his own teeth and a fine physique. He must be close to sixty. She walked over to the mirror. Look at me. Thinning hair, no bottom teeth and skin like a withered prune. What did he expect after all this time? I was no more than thirty when he last saw me. She closed her eyes. She used to be the real glamour girl then, never went out the door without make-up. Now she can't even bother with lipstick.

'You still like a drink, don't you, May?' was one of the first questions Nick had asked.

She opened her eyes, then went to fill the kettle. Yes, she used to like a drink. Saturday nights at Kibbles Wine Bar in Birmingham. After a few drinks there, she'd always go to the cinema. You could enjoy a smoke inside them then, before the days of paranoid lobby groups. How things had changed.

Nick had brought some photos, yellowed and creased with age. He'd slapped one down. 'Remember her?' It was a young May in a pillar-box hat, suit and stilettos.

She gave it a cursory glance.

'You know you used to look a helluva lot like Joan…'

'Who?' She stared at him.

'You know,' he clicked his fingers, 'that actress who was in lots of them old films, never a hair out of place.'

'You mean Crawford?' She handed him back the photo.

'Yeah, he grinned. 'You were the spitting image of her.'

May didn't agree, but she was much too tired to argue.

'I'm married again, you know,' he announced. 'Me and Julie have a daughter and a grandson. Ben's four now. Cheeky little scallywag. He makes me feel young again. It's great having kids around, isn't it?'

'I wouldn't know. I never had any.'

He yawned. May was on the verge of retorting. Don't you ever think about your other wife? Other child? Was it a girl, boy, twins even? You'll never know. Do you even care?

He drummed his fingers on the table. 'You got a nice place here.' He gazed around the room.

'It suits me.'

He cleared his throat. 'I was in the Merchant Navy for years. Had to retire, though. My back started playing up. Can't do any heavy lifting.'

Don't expect any sympathy from me, she mused. A bad back is nothing compared to two miscarriages and a husband who died leaving me with all his gambling debts.

Nick looked at his watch. 'Well, I'd better be going.' He pulled a slip of paper from his pocket. 'Here's our address if you ever want to call in.'

'Oh,' she began to rise, 'I don't want to impose.'

'Don't be daft, May, you won't be imposing. We'd love to have you visit, talk about the old days, eh, except…we're a bit snowed under at the moment,' he looked away, 'getting the kitchen renovated. There's mess everywhere.' He gave her a peck on the cheek and left.

May switched on the kettle. Then, with unsteady fingers, undid the buttons on her blouse. Tentatively she slid a hand across her right breast. The lump was definitely getting bigger. Perhaps that's why she felt so listless. She really should go and see about it. After all, she had a family to consider now.

Or did she? The slip of paper was still on the table. May picked it up, paused, then slowly tore it into small pieces.

Fair Exchange

Skye sat by the window. The café was almost empty, except for a young man in the far corner and an elderly woman who kept patting her lips with a serviette. She ordered a pot of tea and raisin toast. Boring, but safe, especially with the recent increase of food poisoning cases.

A sudden voice startled Skye as she rummaged inside her bag.

'Mind if I join you?'

She looked up. He sat down before she could reply. She was too surprised at first to say anything, sensing the disapproving gaze of the old woman and the grin from the young man.

The stranger studied the menu, quite unperturbed. Skye frowned. Who does he think he is parking himself at my table? She stared out the window. He'll soon get the hint, she thought. She caught a whiff of aftershave.

'Nice place this, isn't it?' He had a cockney accent. His thinning hair was flattened with gel, bushy eyebrows met across the bridge of his wide nose.

The waitress hovered by the table. He ordered a poached egg and chips.

Skye bit into her toast. It wasn't safe speaking to someone she didn't know. And he had a hide to sit down without even asking her. She had to admit he looked harmless enough, somewhere in his sixties, maybe more.

He rubbed at a stain on his jacket's sleeve. 'Just been doing my shopping. I always come into town of a Thursday. Gave my sister in England a ring last night, don't have a phone, go to my neighbour's house.'

She poured her tea. It didn't seem right to ignore him. 'Are you from London?'

'Yes,' he chuckled. 'How'd you guess? Been here more than thirty years. Long before you was born, I'll bet.'

Skye was thrilled with the compliment. She couldn't imagine a time when anybody had ever bothered to praise her. Make her feel special.

He offered her some chips. She refused politely.

'Must watch the figure, eh.' He patted his waist. 'You know, there's one thing I don't ever want to lose and that's me hair,' he tugged at a strand, 'and 'me accent.'

Skye couldn't help smiling.

'I'm real worried about Clara, though, real worried.' He sighed.

'Clara?' She pushed aside her plate.

'Me sister in England, the one I told you I rang. Doctors only give her weeks to live.'

Skye found it difficult to swallow her tea. 'What's wrong with her if you don't mind me asking?'

'Oh, some type of cancer.'

She murmured a few clichéd phrases that even sounded hollow to her.

'There's only the two of us, you know, Clara and me. We were – I mean, are – close. And I got nobody out here.' He sprinkled pepper on his egg.

'Isn't there anybody at all? No friends?'

He shook his head. He must be so lonely. No wonder he was so keen to sit with her.

He waved a chip. 'I can't stand them green. Now where was I…'

'You were telling me that you had nobody here,' Skye prompted him.

'Oh yes, well, I came out here in 1970, been a painter and decorator all me life, retired now. Me name's Sidney. And yours is…?'

'Skye.'

They shook hands. She waited for the inevitable, having always been teased about her name. She hated it.

'You've got a beautiful name. Most girls in my day got called Mary, Debbie, or just plain old Jane, but you should feel real proud.'

He finished his meal, then ordered a coffee and a piece of chocolate cake.

Skye sat up straight. Sidney was the first person to tell her that she had such a beautiful name.

'I got meself a granny flat,' he laughed, 'or should I say a granddad flat at Balmain, right near the water. I can go anywhere all day with my pensioner excursion ticket.'

A few people had entered the café.

'I've been back to England twice, but can't stand that bloomin' cold, though.' He gave a mock shiver. 'I go to see Clara. You ever been to the UK?'

'No,' said Skye, not wanting to elaborate on the fact that she had never been anywhere.

'On my way back from England last time, I called in on Egypt.'

Skye, having once studied Egyptology, was fascinated.

'I went along the Nile on that boat the um…' He clicked his fingers, 'It's on the tip of me tongue…'

She grinned.

'Well, anyway I was on this boat,' he sipped his coffee, marvelling at all this fabulous scenery, and you wouldn't believe where I ended up staying.'

'Where?'

'In this hotel, very posh it were too.' He leaned close to her and whispered, 'I was right next door to where…' he paused, then took a morsel of cake.

'Yes,' urged Skye.

'…to where Agatha Christie slept. She wrote her novel from that very room. *Death on the Nile*. Ever read it?'

She nodded, enthralled waiting for him to continue.

He loosened his tie, relaxed in his chair and spoke, 'That Cairo is teeming, absolutely teeming with people, everywhere. Little kids begging outside hotels, thieves and spiffs. Nearly got robbed twice.' He snatched a look at his watch. 'Gotta go soon. Don't time get away?'

Skye tried to think of something to say that could delay him, when he said, 'I got the flu there didn't I and never felt so ill in my life. Managed to get to a chemist, must have looked a right sight. The staff didn't speak any English and I couldn't speak any Arabic or French.'

'So what happened.?'

'Well, there we were all trying to get through to one another, doing all kinds of complicated gestures, when this bloke in a white coat gives me a tablet.'

'So you took it, then?' Her eyes widened.

Sidney guffawed, 'Course I did, didn't have much choice. I took it as soon as I got back to the hotel.'

'And then what happened.?'

'I blacked out. When I woke up, didn't know where I was but I felt much better. Wouldn't be surprised if it was one of them miracle potions.' He glanced at his watch again.

She was reluctant to let him go. She wanted to know more about him. More about his travels, and his adventures.

Sidney wiped his mouth. 'I should go now. Got some packing to do.' He stood.

'Oh, are you going on another holiday?'

'No. Wished I was. Me old ticker's been playing up. Got to go into hospital tomorrow for an op. A double bypass.'

She didn't know what to say. First his sister very ill, now him. They shook hands before he left the café.

I should have found out what hospital he'll be having the operation in. I could go and visit him. Someone, even a stranger, was better than nobody at all.

The waitress began to clear the table. 'He's a friendly old man, isn't he?'

'Yes,' replied Skye, as she picked up the bills.

That was odd, Sidney must have forgotten to pay for his share. Come to think of it, he was in a bit of a hurry.

The waitress said, 'I couldn't help but overhear him telling you his name was Sidney.'

'Yes, that's right. Why?' Skye took out her purse.

'Because he was in here last week calling himself Bert.'

Contradictions

Kasey knocks at the door, waits a moment, knocks again. The door opens a fraction.

Matted hair and a shrivelled face peers out. 'Yes, darling, can I help you?'

'Good afternoon, Mrs Issacs. I'm Kasey Dawson, your carer for today.' She produces identification.

There is a moment or two of hesitation before the door opens wider, 'Oh, yes, come in. And won't you call me Elishka.'

She leads the way into an almost bare living room. There is a cardboard box filled with crockery, a yellowish sheet thrown across a sofa and two suitcases.

'I'm moving soon, that's why my stuff is packed,' says Elishka as she tucks her collar-length hair beneath a baseball cap.

There are no curtains on any of the windows, except for a sheet of paper taped across one of the panes. The words read, 'This is a non-smoking zone.' An odour of dampness reeks the air.

'You don't smoke, do you?' Elishka narrows her eyes.

'No, I don't.' Kasey replies, noting an ashtray full of butts.

Elishka mumbles something and gestures to Kasey. They make their way through a dim hallway, then into the kitchen.

'Sit down, darling.' Elishka potters about the room. Unwashed pots, plates and utensils litter the table. She removes her baseball cap and throws it onto the nearby sideboard.

'What would you like to drink?' she asks, but before Kasey can respond, she holds up a jar of coffee and a box of Weetbix. 'I've only got these.'

'Coffee will be fine, thanks.' Kasey notices the fridge door is ajar.

'It doesn't work.' Elishka pours boiled water into the mugs.

Kasey feigns surprise. 'What doesn't work?'

'The fridge. I saw you looking.' She gives a sly grin. 'It costs too much to fix it. I don't buy much food. Nothing keeps.' She brings over the coffees. 'There's no milk. You'll have to take it black.' Elishka pushes across the sugar bowl. 'I stay in bed a lot, that's the only way to stay warm. I wish I could offer you some cake or biscuits. Do you think you can bring me something sweet next time?'

Kasey feels squeamish. I'll have to organise meals on wheels for her. 'Um yes, I'll bring you something sweet next time. Would you like anything in particular?'

'Oh, anything tasty.' Elishka scratches her hair. 'So how long have you been doing this work?'

'Six months or thereabouts. It's great, better than being stuck in an office.'

'How old are you?'

'Thirty.'

'Aren't you married?' Elishka stares at Kasey's ringless fingers.

'No.'

'Why not? What's wrong? An attractive girl like you should be married.'

'I guess I just haven't met the right man yet.' Kasey decides to do some quizzing herself. 'So how long ago did your husband die?'

'Twelve months. My Hyme was a wonderful man and so clever. He was going to write a book about the environment and how we're destroying it with all these chemicals. I'm a vegetarian. It's criminal to see the land used for cattle when we should be growing food on it.' She goes across to the sideboard, snatches a photo out of an album and passes it to Kasey.

She gazes at a dark-haired man with a bushy moustache.

'My Hyme died for nothing. Nothing. They killed him.' She grabs Kasey's arm.

'Who killed him?' Kasey shifts to the edge of the chair.

'Those rotten doctors at the hospital!' She spits. Her eyes bulge. 'He only went there for some tests. He was feeling a bit tired. I'm sure they experimented on him.' Her voice sounds hoarse. She loosens her grip on Kasey's arm.

'How long was he in hospital?'

'Not even a week. He looked terrible. I should've done something.'

Kasey swallows. Is this just an old woman's rambling?

Silence. The clock ticks. A vinegar fly buzzes around Kasey's head.

Suddenly, Elishka roars, bangs her fist on the table. 'I'm going to sue those doctors for negligence. They aren't going to get away with murdering my husband.' Elishka leans across the table. 'I've got a proposition for you, darling.' She takes a long pause. 'How would you like to come into business with me?'

Kasey's mouth is agape.

'Well, are you interested?' Elishka's dirty fingernails rap on the table.

'Um, I don't know. I'ld need to think about it.'

'What's there to think about! It's simple. I'm going to start a sandwich delivery business and supply all the factories and offices in the area. We can make the sandwiches and sell them for ten dollars each.'

Kasey is still coming to terms with this proposal when Elishka asks, 'Do you have a car?'

'No, I don't drive.'

'Oh, never mind,' she snaps. 'It's just that we need our own transport. We'll have to hire a taxi and claim on tax.' She rubs her hands.

Kasey is dumbfounded. One minute Elishka is wailing over the death of her husband, the next she is planning to start a sandwich business.

'Me and Hyme were pastry cooks, we had our own shop, but had to sell it when he started to feel tired.'

Kasey stares at those fingernails. Did Elishka bother to keep them clean when she was in the pastry business?

'So when can you start?' Elishka runs a tongue around her lips.

Kasey clears her throat. 'It's a bit too soon for me to decide, with my home visits and all. I'll let you know.' Is Elishka serious about this sandwich business? Maybe I'll just humour her. It could be a story.

Elishka reaches across and snatches a Weetbix from the box.

Kasey fidgets, thinks she ought to say something, *anything*. 'Do you have any children?'

Elishka stops munching her Weetbix. 'Yes, one son, Jacob. He went to Israel. He's studying to become a rabbi. Rabbi bah.' She rocks back and forth, then throws up her hands. 'We always told him he was wasting his life.' She yawns.

There is a loud thud, sounds as if it's coming from upstairs.

Kasey looks at Elishka. 'What's that?'

'What, darling?' She takes another Weetbix.

'That loud noise, didn't you hear it?'

'Oh, that. It's only the possums.'

'Possums?'

'Yes, I've got lots in my roof.'

More like possums in army boots. Kasey couldn't help but be a little curious. A moment or two elapses.

'Can I use your bathroom, please?'

'Yes, go ahead, it's upstairs, second on your right.'

Inside the bathtub is a scrunched-up shower curtain. A few dark hairs surround the sink. On the windowsill is a bloodstained, or is it a rusted, syringe? And what about those hairs? Who do they belong to? Elishka's hair is grey. Kasey quickly rinses her hands and wipes them on the back of her jeans. There is no towel. Another thud, louder this time. She decides not to mention the syringe and the strange noises. Obviously Elishka is not alone. But what is she hiding and why? Kasey swallows. This place is creepy. She returns to the kitchen.

Elishka is making herself another coffee. 'Do you know anybody who wants accommodation?'

'No, I don't. Why?' She sits down, cursing herself. She should've taken a look in the other rooms.

'I want to get in boarders. A girl came to see the room, but she was too fussy. She wanted a heater and hot water! I've got the tank switched off. I boil my water when I want to wash. Once, I had a young man stay with me. Told me his grandfather was German. I kicked him out.'

Kasey glances at her watch. 'I really have to get going now.'

'Oh, darling, don't go yet.' Elishka reaches across and grabs Kasey's hand, 'You're the best company I've had for a long time. Sometimes I don't get to see anybody for weeks.'

'Oh, all right, but only for a little while.'

Elishka crosses her legs, then settles into her chair. 'My husband and I arrived in Australia just after the war. We were very lucky to escape the Hitler camps.' She uncrosses her legs and leans closer to Kasey. 'The churches knew what was happening, but they did nothing. Absolutely nothing to stop the slaughter of innocent civilians. They were all hypocrites.' She wipes a frail hand across her eyes and gives a sniff. In between sobs, she speaks about the fear, displacement of friends, neighbours, the hatreds against her people.

Kasey does not interrupt.

Elishka comes to an abrupt halt. She sits motionless. 'You know, I've never talked like this to anybody, not even to my son.' Kasey nods and places a hand lightly on her shoulder. Eishka gives her a watery smile.

The phone rings. Seconds slide.

'Aren't you going to answer it?'

'Oh, it'll only be someone wanting to sell me something. I get those calls all the time, drives me crazy. Did I tell you that I was moving soon?' says Elishka.

'Yes,' Kasey smiles. 'You told me earlier.'

'I've been trying to sell this place for over a year. The agent wants me to renovate. Renovate. What for! The house is in perfect condition.' Elishka stands then shuffles over to the sink. Loose threads cling to her green slacks. 'Darling,' she speaks, keeps her back to Kasey, 'I've got some DVDs to sell. Do you know anybody who might buy them?'

'What are they about?'

'The're all on the body.' She returns to the table, avoids eye contact with Kasey.

'The body? Oh, like biology docos?'

'Not exactly. It's the type that men get pleasure from watching.'

'You mean porn?' Kasey wants to explode with laughter, but manages to keep a straight face.

Elishka chuckles. 'I'm selling the lot for a hundred dollars. A bargain.'

'Whose were they?'

'My Hyme's of course. He'd invite his friends over, have a few drinks, then watch the films.'

'I'm afraid I don't know of anyone who'd be interested.'

There is more racket from above.

'Did you hear…' Kasey begins.

Elishka stands. 'I must go to bed now. I'm feeling a little tired.' She ushers Kasey towards the front hall. 'Now, darling, don't forget to bring me something sweet next time, won't you?' She gives her a gentle push before closing the door.

I'll make sure Elishka gets all the assistance she needs. I wonder if her son realises she's living in such deplorable conditions. She must be very lonely.

Kasey is halfway down the path when she hears a noise and spins round. A head pops out of an upstairs window. And he is crying. She is about to wave, but he disappears. Who is he? Could it be Hyme? She must do something. Kasey takes a deep breath, is about to pull out her mobile when a smartly dressed man opens the front gate and approaches her.

'Hello, can I help you?' he asks.

'I'm Kasey Dawson, Mrs Issacs's carer, and you are?'

'I'm Jacob.'

They shake hands.

'Oh, you must be her son. She told me that you were studying to be a rabbi.'

'Rabbi! Ha, that'll be the day. She's crazy. Keeps my dad locked upstairs like a prisoner.'

'So that's the man I saw at the window.'

'Yep, that's him all right. I'm in real estate and trying to get Mum to sell this place. She's getting worse and can't look after Dad any more. I keep ringing her, but she never answers the phone. You were lucky that she let you in. She's suspicious of everybody.'

'She told me that your father's dead.' Kasey grimaces.

'Oh, Mum tells that story to everyone.'

The front door opens.

'He's not my son. Don't believe a word he says. He's a conman,' Elishka screeches.

The door bangs shut.

He fidgets with his right ear lobe. 'Who do you believe?' Jacob shifts his gaze.

Friend or Foe

It's uncanny how I can remember *exactly* what I was doing when tragedy occurred. I was watering my plants. The phone rang. It was Vicky's daughter, Ellie, telling me in a cool voice that her mother was dead. She had been stabbed. The cleaner had discovered the body that morning. Robbery was not a motive. There was no forced entry. I was horrified, felt squeamish. Who would do such a thing? I poured myself a large brandy.

I had to be honest; Vicky had never been an easy person. I'd even had my share of quarrels with her. We'd arrived from Greece almost thirty years before, both petite brunettes, but that's where the similarities ended. She was far more attractive and I had always been a little jealous of her. Vicky had everything, looks, money and a daughter. We hadn't been close, but I expect growing up in the same village gave us something in common. A link to the hardships of the past.

Whenever we went to parties, Vicky was, without exception, the gregarious one. 'C'mon, you'll have such fun.' She'd glide around the room in a low-cut tight-fitting dress.

Once after a few drinks, I told her how cute I thought her husband was. Her reaction was to give a brittle laugh. She'd been married twice. Her first husband, a property developer had died; this second husband George was much younger and better-looking.

I made an unexpected visit to her place one afternoon. Vicky was out and George insisted I come in and wait. My biggest mistake. Soon one glass of wine became two, then three and before long we moved from the divan to the bedroom. Two uninterrupted hours of pure lust. We never repeated the episode and in less than a month George had disappeared. Maybe he felt guilty. I wanted to tell Vicky about our liaison, but there never seemed to be the right moment. Or was I making excuses? I certainly didn't make a habit of snatching other women's husbands.

The strange thing was Vicky didn't speak about George. It was as though he never existed.

And she'd recently disowned her daughter when Ellie got pregnant. I remembered Vicky's rage. 'She should've got rid of it. A good career ahead of her. Stupid girl. I don't know what I've done to deserve such an ungrateful daughter. All that money I've spent on her university fees.' She had been eager for sympathy. I offered none.

Last night I went to see Vicky. I couldn't live with my conscience any more. I planned to confide in her about my fling with George. She already knew, called me names, then slapped me across the face. I slapped her back. We had a scuffle, and she seemed all right when I left, apart from a few scratches. Despite our wrangle, I could've sworn I heard somebody moving about upstairs.

The police would investigate Vicky's murder. I'd have to tell them the reason for our argument. I was bound to be a suspect. My fingerprints were all over her place. I'd be blamed. Nobody would believe me, especially when my bed-hopping with George was revealed.

There was a sudden noise, probably next door's cat. I'd left the back screen open. I'd check on it later. Greece in spring sounded ideal. I could lie low for a while. Disguise myself. I was about to ring the travel agent when a hand clamped on my shoulder. I spun round.

George stood there. 'Going somewhere, darling? I think we've got some talking to do.'

Vicky's daughter stood beside him.

'Did you know that I'm about to be a daddy soon?' He patted Ellie's stomach.

'A pity poor mother couldn't have been around for the happy event.' Ellie gave me a smug smile.

Blackberry Blues

'Teeth and legs,' I say.

'What?' Beloved asks.

'Teeth and legs, that's what I first noticed about Mirrabella. No wonder she became a pole dancer. Last night she went out in a red mini-skirt. Someone picked her up in a sports car.'

Mirrabella, of the viper tongue and tulip lips, is my next-door neighbour.

'But isn't she a grandmother?' He erupts on his raspberry tea.

'Yeah, granny by day, pole dancer by night.' I brush grass stems from my jeans.

'What! Truly, honestly?' His jaw drops.

'Oh, I don't know.' He can be so naïve at times.

At this moment, Mirrabella walks past.

'She's a right cow anyway,' I hiss.

'Be quiet! She can hear you,' Beloved says.

I shrug. We are in my front garden, where all good neighbourly battles begin.

First, there was the three-foot picket fence, which in time became a six-foot one, aptly named the Berlin Wall. Mirrabella demanded her privacy and, with council on side, got her own way.

Second was the battle over her hedges that had encroached onto my property. Beloved became a little too rampant with the trimmer one day and hacked into the hedges, resulting in near baldness. Ever since, there has been the occasional snipe, followed by months of silence.

Neddy is my other next-door neighbour. Earlier this morning, Beloved, with permission from Neddy, cut back his obnoxious blackberry vine. It had created a stained mess all over my front brick fence.

As we grab another bottle of sugar soap to clean it, I say, 'I bet Neddy's off cycling somewhere.'

'Yeah,' he pants. 'It's all right for him!'

Three hours and a lot of sweat later, the task is complete.

'I reckon I did a *berry* good job.' He grins, standing back to admire his work.

I roll my eyes.

That evening I stay at Beloved's place. We light incense sticks, play snakes and ladders and drink copious amounts of ginger tea.

The following night as soon as Poirot arrests his suspect, he drives me home. The sensor light flicks on and off as I make my way up to the front door. Dirt and branches scatter the path. Strange, I think, there hasn't been a storm.

Then I notice my small Geisha Girl torn from its roots. 'What the hell's happened here?' I shriek, running over to my mangled tree.

'A case for Poirot perhaps?' says Beloved.

'It's not funny! Who would do such a vicious thing?' I kneel beside it.

'C'mon, let's go inside.' He places an arm around my shoulder.

As I am about to insert my key into the security door, I give a loud gasp.

'What now!'

'Look!' I point a trembling finger at the door handle. 'Somebody's broken it.'

He moves me gently aside, stares at the mutilated handle, then gives a low whistle. 'Where's the rest of it?' Beloved strokes his chin. 'Bound to be DNA on it.'

'Oh yeah. What's the use of that if it's gone? Whoever did this took it with them. The same person or persons who destroyed my tree. Now I've only got half a door handle. Lovely.' I fume. 'Apparently, they didn't care who saw them, as my sensor light would've been going on and off. It must have taken them a while to mutilate the handle. How bizarre.'

I open my front door and step inside. Racing through the hall, I switch on all the lights, taking a peep in every room.

'Just what are you doing?' Beloved gives me one of his quirky looks.

'Checking in case there's somebody hiding.'

He then goes and tests all my windows and the back door. 'I bet it was that Mirrabella. She did it on purpose, overheard you calling her a cow. I told you to keep your voice down,' he admonishes me.

'So now I'm to blame.' I want to hurl my large swede at him.

'OK, OK.' He scratches his head. 'What about Neddy? I did cut his tree back.'

'But he gave us permission, remember. We've been neighbours for years. Never a cross word between us.'

'He even offered to chase an ex of mine who'd been snooping around.'

'When was this?' Beloved's mouth falls open like a clown at a funfair.

I give a sigh, 'Oh, Ormond was in the street recently, but I wasn't at home.'

'And?' He raises an eyebrow.

'He spotted Neddy in his garden, approached him and began to ask questions about me, like was I still single? Did I have a boyfriend?'

'Bastard!' he spat. 'It must've been him.'

'I doubt it. Ormond's not the violent type.'

'Sounds like you're defending him.' He collapses onto my sofa and runs a hand through his hair.

I continue. 'Ormond is very immature in many ways. I guess he never grew up. This kind of weird behaviour is not his style, but...'

Beloved sits up straight, shifts to the edge of the sofa. 'But...' he prompts me.

I avert my gaze. 'I took an AVO out on him.'

'Ah ha, so he was violent, then?'

'No, but there were persistent phone calls. He wouldn't get it through his head that I didn't want to see him any more. He even came to my door once and was quite irrational. I think he'd been drinking.'

He snorts. 'And you reckon this guy has nothing to do with your mangled tree and missing door handle.'

'But we broke up a fair while ago.'

'People hold grudges. After all, there was your AVO.'

I swallow, then begin to fill the kettle. 'Anyway, that's all in the past. I've got to deal with the present by reporting this horrible incident to the police.'

'Police! Is that really necessary?'

'Of course it is. Someone has vandalised my property.' My voice rises.

He comes over and gives me a hug 'Yeah, well, if it eases your mind, call them tomorrow. At least then they'll have a record of it.'

I make each of us a cup of chamomile tea. 'It will calm me down. But I could do with something stronger.'

He glances at his watch. 'Too late. Bottle shops have closed.'

I stir a teaspoon of honey into my tea. 'You know, what if it was Neddy?'

'So why not ask him and also ask some of the other neighbours.'

About half an hour later, Beloved yawns, 'Gotta go. My girls will be wondering where I am.' The girls being his two cheeky Siamese cats. 'But will you be all right? I don't like to leave you on your own. Come back to my place.'

'No, I'll be fine. I'm sure whoever did this has long gone. I mean, they wouldn't hang around a crime scene.'

'Crime scene!' Beloved explodes with laughter. 'You've been watching too much of that Poirot.'

'It is a crime scene, a throttled tree and a piece of door handle that's gone AWOL.'

He kisses me on the forehead. 'Give me a ring if you change your mind.'

I rinse the cups, brush my teeth quickly, then dive beneath the bed-clothes. Stillness, except for the ticking from my wind-up clock.

I switch off my bedside lamp, then switch it on again. I sit up and throw off a blanket. The tick, tick, tick disturbs me. Beloved is forever telling me to toss it out, go digital. The same way he tries to persuade me to buy a computer, mobile phone. My thoughts spin like a dodgem car out of control.

The incident in my front garden is baffling, alarming even. What if it is Ormond? I'd have to organise another AVO. Go to court again. I lie down and switch off the lamp. Turning on my side, I snuggle into the pillow and close my eyes.

Early the next morning, I search my front garden, but fail to find the missing door handle piece. Afterwards, I call the police.

'Malicious damage is a serious offence,' says an officer with a gruff but kind voice.

I feel so much better for having reported it.

I ask some of my neighbours, but they claim they didn't see or hear anything unusual. Mirrabella gives me a smirk whenever she goes past me.

Three days later, I come across Neddy. I tell him about the incident.

His response floors me, 'So now we're even.' He undoes the straps from his bike helmet.

'What!' I almost choke. My chest tightens. 'How dare you stoop to such tactics. It's not only childish, but very vindictive. I really thought someone was trying to break into my house.'

'Your partner destroyed my beautiful blackberry vine. He cut it back far too much.' His face is fire-truck red.

I snap, 'But we did seek your permission first. That so called beautiful vine was making a huge mess all over my fence. We spent hours removing the stains. And anyway, if it is a case of an eye for an eye, how come you broke my security door handle?'

He frowns. His small eyes squint. 'I never touched your door handle.'

'Ha, you expect me to believe that after what you did. I've reported it to the police, but I couldn't name the offender then.' I glare at him.

'My vine is very precious to me.'

'I should make you pay for the damage to my door handle.'

'But I told you I never touched it.'

I don't believe him. He doesn't apologise.

That night, I call Beloved and tell him Neddy is the culprit.

'Aren't you going to press charges?' he asks.

'No, it'll only complicate matters and he could do something worse. It was strange how he kept denying the damage to my door handle, though. Why not just admit to it?'

'It only goes to prove that he's a liar as well as a bastard. You know I keep telling you to rent out your house and move in with me. I've got great neighbours.'

Yes I muse, including the man next door who has a tattooed face and a house full of wigs.

The following day there is a small gift wrapped item inside my letter box. I unwrap it to discover my missing door handle piece.

I hear a sudden noise and glance up. Mirrabella, in black fishnet stockings, hurries over to a revving car.

Ormond is at the wheel. He gives me a wave.

My Man Charlie

'They should all be exterminated,' said Warwick as he took another swig of wine. By 'they', he meant people who were homeless, or unemployed. Those who didn't conform to his standards.

We'd been discussing the kinds of people living on the edge, either by choice, or circumstance. I looked at Zita. She raised her over-plucked eyebrows. No wonder his wife had left him, I thought. What was I doing in his local anyway? I would've been better off staying home with Charlie.

Introducing Zita to Warwick was maybe not such a brilliant idea. She had been pestering me for weeks to arrange a date. He wasn't bad-looking; slim forty-something of average height, dark hair and a thin moustache. Zita wore a frilly blouse, short skirt and too much make-up. I felt at ease in my jeans, T-shirt and unwashed hair. I wasn't here to make an impression on anyone. Warwick went to fetch another carafe of wine.

Zita was quiet. I wasn't game to ask her whether she was disappointed. The first time I'd met Warwick and his ex-wife Marla was at my local tennis courts. We used to play twice a week, but I grew tired of his boasting and his tantrums. He returned to the table. I shook my head when he offered more wine. Two was my limit.

'You know she' – he never used Marla's name – 'would go berserk just because my jackets and shirts weren't all facing the same way in the wardrobe. And she wanted to throw out my valuable antique collection.'

'So you have antiques?' Zita moved closer to the table.

'Well, not exactly antiques,' he stroked his chin, 'but they will be one day. You should come over and see them.'

His valuable collection consisted of several wind-up clocks, stacks of tattered paperbacks and a manual typewriter with missing keys. He never threw out anything. I decided not to disillusion her. She would find out soon enough.

'And she never came ghost hunting with me either.'

'Ghost hunting!' Zita yelled, then glanced around to see if anyone had heard.

'Yes, I've been to a few graveyards after midnight hoping to spot a ghost.'

'Did you ever see one?' Zita's mouth was agape.

'No, but I'm still hoping. Would you like to come one night?'

'I'd love to but I'd be too scared unless we all…' She looked at me, 'Would you…'

I refused. Visiting graveyards was a foolish deed I once did as a teenager. I never came across any ghosts, but had tripped and sprained my ankle.

Warwick began to tell Zita about his many trips to Bali. I gave a yawn, wondering what Charlie was up to.

'Bali?' she sighed. 'I've always wanted to go there. Do you think you'll ever go again.'

'Oh, I might with the right sort of company.' He replenished her glass.

His wife had left him three months before. Had he forgotten her already?

'If you ever get to Bali, Zita, you'll have to try their omelettes.'

'Why?'

I knew what to expect. I'd heard it all before.

'They put psychedelic mushrooms in them.'

'What!' she laughed. 'Are you kidding?'

'I got high after only eating a small piece. Me and my mate Arnold had a terrific time there. You'll definitely have to meet him.'

A confirmed bachelor at almost forty-five, Arnold's idea of a good night out was a cheap meal at his local bowling club followed by a monologue on the Napoleanic Wars. One date had been enough for me.

'You'll have to bring Zita to my brother's barbecue this Sunday,' said Warwick.

I made no comment. His brother was an alcoholic and on the verge of losing his job. Too many liquid lunches.

'Thought I'd find you in here,' sang out a familiar voice.

We turned.

It was Marla. She nodded to me, sat down and gave Zita an indifferent look. 'I've been thinking, darl. How about I move back in and we give things another go, hey?' She leaned across and ruffled Warwick's hair.

I stood. 'Well, I'd better go. Got to get home and see to Charlie.'

'Charlie!' they all exclaimed.

'Got a new man in your life?' asked Marla.

'Yeah, and he isn't hooked on psychedelic mushrooms either.'

'Well, c'mon, spill the beans,' grinned Warwick.

'So who is this new guy of yours?' Zita fingered her wine glass.

I turned and headed towards the exit, not bothering to tell them that Charlie was my new budgie.

Lipstick Lullaby

'Nerida and Donald are a fantastic couple,' says Risa during one of our recent phone conversations.

'How did you meet them?' I ask.

'We met at a cocktail party in Buenos Aires.'

I envy her job as a cosmetic consultant. She is forever travelling to some exotic destination.

'She's Argentinian and he's American. Their apartment is gorgeous, it overlooks the water. We went out to dinner and I also spent a week at their ranch. Don owns racehorses.'

'How wonderful.' I feign enthusiasm, feeling a little jealous.

'And now it's my turn to repay their hospitality.'

'What do you mean?'

'They want to spend a fortnight in Sydney, stay with me.'

'But you hardly know them.' Risa could be so naïve at times.

'I guess I had too many tequilas when they asked if they could stay.'

Risa and I have been close friends for almost six months. She was there for me when I'd been made redundant. She helped me with my debts and even bought me meals and drinks whenever we went out. We revealed everything to each other, like the time I got away with passport forging.

'I'd love you to meet them. I'll cook your favourite. What do you say?'

Vegetarian lasagne sounds tempting, but I hesitate. 'Oh, I don't know, Risa. You know me. I hate meeting new people and having to make small talk.'

'Oh, c'mon. There a fun couple. You'll like them.'

Before the night of the dinner, I decide not to stay long and to invent an excuse to leave soon after dessert. Taking a deep breath, I ring the front door bell.

'They can't wait to meet you.' Risa embraces me.

We enter the dining room. A smartly dressed couple approach me.

'Call me Don,' he grins, giving my hand a vigorous shake.

'I'm Nerida.' She brushes my cheek with her lips. 'Pleased to meet you.' She toys with her silver bracelet. Her dark upswept hair is adorned with pretty combs. She's at least twenty years his junior.

Don wipes his flushed face. Blood pressure, or is it the heat? I muse.

The table is laid with Old Country Roses, a bottle of Hermitage 1982 and strawberry-scented candles.

Don shrugs off his jacket and loosens his tie. We sit down.

'How are you enjoying your stay?' I ask him.

'Terrific. You gotta beautiful harbour and them beaches are just something else. There's a whole lot more we wanna see yet, isn't there, babe?' He pats Nerida's hand.

She flinches. 'I'm not crazy about beaches and all that sun can't be any good for one's complexion.' She straightens a comb.

Risa places the lasagne before Don and me while she and Nerida have salads.

Where is this fun couple Risa boasts about? Except for Don making the odd mundane comment, or Nerida asking me to pass her the salt, we eat in silence.

About twenty or so minutes later, Risa leaps up. 'I'll go fetch the desserts.' She scurries into the kitchen.

Don reclines in his chair. 'Risa tells me you're outta work, finding it hard to get by.'

'Yes, that's right,' I reply. His shrewd gaze disturbs me. 'I'll just go and see if Risa needs any help.'

Nerida's grip on my arm prevents me from rising. 'She'll be fine.'

Don strokes his chin. 'We have a proposition for you. Nerida and I have our own cosmetic company, Lipstick Lulluby, and we'd like to offer you a job on our team. Risa's been with us for years, she's practically running the company.'

I am stunned. So Risa is their employee. Why did she pretend that she met them at a cocktail party? And why all the secrecy?

'Lullaby isn't your average cosmetic,' he says.

'What do you mean?'

Risa enters with the desserts. 'He means…'

'Let Don do the talking, darling.' Nerida glares at Risa.

He clears his throat. 'The lipstick cases are used to conceal amounts of…shall we call it medicine.'

'Medicine?' I repeat, wishing he'd get to the point.

'Heroin, darling. We arrange your flights, accommodation, contacts. And we take a percentage.'

Nerida gives me a cryptic smile.

Risa the drug smuggler. No wonder she is rolling in dosh.

'Hear you gotta talent for forging. We sure could use your kinda skills,' says Don.

How could Risa betray me? What else has she told them?

Don snaps his fingers. I jump. Nerida lights a cigarette, takes a puff, then hands it to Risa.

'Look, I'll have to think about this. It's not exactly your average job, is it?'

Don licks the back of his ice cream coated spoon, 'What's stopping you?'

'Getting caught for one.'

'Getting caught! Thought it was your damn conscience for a minute. No need to worry on that score, honey. We got all our bases covered.' He winks. 'Been in the game too long.'

I glance at Risa. She averts her eyes. Months of drawing information out of me, learning about my past, grooming me for her bosses. A new recruit.

I swallow. The money is tempting. And I do have a tendency to live on the edge, especially after my stint as a forger.

'Yeah, you have a think about it.' Don puts an arm around Nerida. 'But don't take too long.'

Risa walks me to the door. 'It's a job in a million. You get to travel, meet people, stay in luxurious hotels.' She opens the door. Whispers. 'Go for it. What have you got to lose.'

I step into the scalding night air.

Envy

I never met the Sick Lady but felt as though I knew her.

Renata often spoke about her and was forever going to her house. 'The Sick Lady loves me like a daughter, cooks for me, treats me like a queen. We picked some snake beans from her garden yesterday.' Renata clasped her hands, giving me her cryptic smile.

This friend, I'd recently discovered, was just overweight and not sick at all. Renata still insisted on calling her the Sick Lady.

'Her husband left her. Men don't like fat women,' said Renata.

I sipped my cappuccino. We'd known each other years – too long, in fact. She was ten years my senior, petite, with a flawless complexion and no grey hair. She would often boast about her good-looking boy-friend whom I'd never met. Renata had no competition from me, not with my mousey hair and large thighs.

I watched her closely as she thinly scraped margarine onto her toast. Mine was thickly spread. So what if I had to take size sixteens instead of twelves. I had nobody to impress and my erstwhile lover was dumped because he'd made snide remarks about my thighs. Renata never knew about him. She'd probably only laugh, surprised to find that I'd even had a lover. She was forever suggesting courses or social groups I should join. It was fine for her to talk with her elegance and money. She had a two-bedroom villa.

I was out of work and lived in a small flat with my mother. Renata had only been to my place once. I expect the sight of unwashed dishes and a cockroach scurrying along the sink was enough to make her bolt.

Occasionally, I'd test her out and ask her to visit me again, but she always invented some excuse. Unlike me, she had no income hassles and must have made a mint on the sale of her parents' estate. Next week, she is going to the Gold Coast for ten days. Renata could have offered to pay for my holiday. I never go anywhere, or do anything. She is the only friend I've got. She only ever asks me out when it suits her. And she's never introduced me to the Sick Lady. Is afraid that I'll snatch her away. I'd love to wander through a garden picking home-grown vegetables. The only bit of grass I ever get to see is in my local park.

We order another coffee. Renata shows me a new pair of earrings. I smile and listen as she chatters about where she bought them and how much they had cost. Whenever we go shopping, or should I say whenever Renata goes shopping, she spends hours trying on clothes, as she laps up compliments from the shop assistants.

'You must come and see my exotic rug one day,' she said.

'What rug?'

She went on to tell me about the five-hundred-dollar rug she'd had delivered last week. 'And I've had my floors polished too.'

Renata had admitted once that she wasn't too keen on encouraging guests. Those who did come had to remove their shoes before they were allowed to enter. 'Don't spill any crumbs, will you?' she had warned me when I first visited her villa, hovering nearby with a broom.

She never cooked, preferring to eat at her boyfriend's, or the Sick Lady's house. What was the point of having your own place if you spent most of your time elsewhere? Wish I could be on my own. Do what I want, when I want. Not have to listen to mother's whines.

'So when are you coming to see my rug?'

I thought for a moment. This could be the perfect opportunity. I might never get another chance. I remembered Renata telling me once how the Sick Lady went sliding on one of her own rugs. Apparently she damaged her hip. Renata said she was a clumsy cow. Rugs and polished floors are not a good mix.

It will be easy. Once Renata's back is turned, I will concoct an accident. Simple. Go for a slide on her rug. There will be some bruising, perhaps a fractured limb or two. I could sue her for my medical expenses. She will have to cancel her trip. Serves her right.

'Well, when are you…' she prompted.

'What about tomorrow?'

Mother

Mother. Dead at last. What a relief, thought Regina. No more abuse, like the time when Mother beat her because Regina had insisted on wearing a red miniskirt.

'You are not leaving my house looking like a harlot,' she spat, then later ripped the garment into shreds. And even worse, Mother threatened to alter her will. 'You are not going to get anything if you disobey me. Not the house, not the money, not my jewellery, nothing!' The taunts were almost daily.

The death certificate stated asphyxiation as the cause. Mother had never been ill in her life. She'd only gone into hospital for some tests as she was worried about persistent chest pains. Next month would have been her seventieth birthday.

Regina remembered there was nobody in the private room when she decided to act. She quickly tore a crusty bread roll into pieces before forcing them into Mother's mouth. Crumbs like confetti littered the blue cotton bedspread. Mother, with terror in her eyes, feebly clawed at Regina's hands. A short time later, she went still, her arms slumped on the counterpane. Regina leaned over to check her breathing and pulse. Just to make sure. She waited a minute or two, then began to scream.

Suddenly, staff emerged swarming around Mother like agitated wasps. Regina sobbed, enjoying the pretence.

'Get this lady some water,' a voice echoed.

Another whispered, 'The old woman's dead.'

That was over a week ago.

Regina smirked at herself in the full-length mirror. Forty and still a virgin, with a flat chest, thin legs and unruly brown hair. Today, she'd make an appointment for a haircut and she might even buy a few padded bras.

'See, Mother,' she said admiring her new pink lipstick, 'you never wanted me to look attractive. You wanted me to stay ugly. Never meet anybody.'

In Mother's opinion, men were lustful creatures like Father, who had deserted them years ago for a much younger woman. Since then, Regina had to live by Mother's rules: no make-up, no boyfriends, and Mass was a must every Sunday. Regina hated the rules, but she lacked both the courage and the finances to live on her own. Life, although restricting in some ways, could also be very comfortable. Regina's only duty was to help with the shopping, as Mother did all the cooking, washing and cleaning.

Regina was forbidden to go anywhere, unless escorted by her uncle. He was too old for Mother to have any misgivings. Once, when he was unable to escort her to the movies, she was taken by her acne-infested cousin. Halfway through the film, he left with a stinging cheek.

'Where's your cousin?' Mother had interrogated Regina on her return. 'He knows that he's supposed to bring you home. I gave him strict instructions.'

'Oh,' said Regina, 'he felt ill and had to leave in a hurry.' She didn't bother to inform Mother that his hand had wandered up her leg.

Regina's only other social outlet was popping into see her next door neighbour, a seamstress with a good-looking son. Regina blushed as she remembered the erotic videos they used to watch and the time when the neighbour was out and her son had exposed himself to her. At first she was horrified by his nakedness, but she soon became engrossed, especially when he began to masturbate.

Funny how Mother thought Regina was learning how to sew.

The phone startled her.

She answered it with some reluctance, expecting it to be one of her teary-eyed relatives. 'Hello.'

'Good morning. Miss Bartucci?'

'Yes, speaking.' The voice was muffled. Regina couldn't tell if it was a male or a female.

'I was one of the staff who attended your mother. I was hoping that we could meet.'

'Meet? What for?' Regina snapped. Who was this?

'It's too delicate a matter to discuss on the phone.'

'I don't understand.'

'Oh, but I think you do. I was there. I saw what you did. You forced that bread down your mother's throat.'

'What! How dare you! My mother choked.' Regina's palms felt sweaty. Her heart raced.

'Are you still there, Miss Bartucci?'

'Yes, I'm here. But you've got it all wrong. I'd never harm my mother. We were very close. I loved her.'

There was a moment or so of silence.

'Shall we arrange a time and place, Miss Bartucci?'

The Reunion

I shouldn't have accepted tonight's invitation to the St Bridget's School reunion. How many women would even be bothered to show up? Had any remained friends since we'd graduated all those years ago? I'd never kept in touch with the girls or the teachers. The rules and rituals were something I'd rather forget.

This reunion was like meeting a group of strangers, all facade and innocuous chatter. Had they remembered my humiliating episodes? When a sister dragged me in front of the class and belted me because I hadn't finished my homework. Or the day when I was made to walk around the playground in the heat, all because I'd forgotten my beret and gloves.

My old classmate June reckoned that nuns were the most sex-starved creatures on earth. They rarely smiled, or showed any emotion. I tended to agree with June, I mean who else applied for a job with the prerequisite of celibacy.

I went down the hall and opened the door to my daughter's bedroom. Inside was a multicoloured beanbag and her guitar in the corner.

Francine was twenty and had left home three months ago to move in with her art teacher, a man twice her age. We'd argued about it, but no amount of reasoning could persuade her to stay. Why couldn't she have met somebody her own age? Somebody who wasn't already married.

Francine's parting words still grated. 'You don't understand, Mum. We love each other and he's so much more mature than any of the guys I know.' She'd shown me his photo on her smart phone, dark hair and moustache.

I stood there for a few moments, blew my nose and blinked. The reunion was for six-thirty. It could always be cancelled, although it might do me good to have a night out. Take my mind off Francine, if only for a short while. I closed her door and returned to my room.

As I dabbed a lightly scented perfume behind my ears, I felt a flutter of excitement. I pulled my brown hair into a chignon, slipped my feet into a pair of black stilettos. I rang for a cab and in less than an hour was entering the Greek restaurant. I stood about awkwardly, until a waiter led me out into the courtyard. Beneath a gnarled tree was a long table with bowls of garlic bread, olives and fetta cheese. Several women stopped their conversation and gazed at me.

'Hello, everybody, I'm Vivian.' My armpits felt damp. I cleared my throat. Perhaps a night in with the TV would have been the better option.

An elderly woman with black hairs sprouting from a double chin shouted, 'What did you say, dear?'

'I'm Vivian, Vivian Sheldon,' I repeated in a louder voice.

'Well, don't just stand there, sit down. Welcome to the St Bridget's reunion,' said Double Chin.

I sighed, feeling like a reprimanded schoolgirl. That had to be my old teacher. A small gold cross was pinned to her jacket. She'd have to be in her seventies now.

There was a tap on my shoulder; I turned.

'Hi, Viv, it's Dora, Dora Reece. How are you? Long time no see.'

We hugged. This wasn't the Dora I remembered. Where was the skinny girl with the mop of curly hair and crooked teeth? This Dora had a stylish bob and perfect teeth. Rings suffocated her plump fingers.

She kept tugging at her tight skirt. 'I used to be a size ten, must have put on weight,' she whispered.

I nodded, glancing along the table. I didn't recognise anyone.

Suddenly there was a whiff of alcohol as somebody leaned over, giving me a peck on the cheek. 'It's June, June Hampton. Great to see you, Viv. You've hardly changed, you look terrific,' said a flush-faced blonde woman.

I stared. There was no trace of the teenager with the pigtails and the cheeky grin. I'd never forget that hilarious incident in the science lab when June had spewed, before we'd even started to dissect the rat.

'Wine, Vivian?' Dora filled her glass then mine.

June raised her glass, 'This is already my fourth.'

Sister sipped her orange juice. I used to be so afraid of her striding along the corridors, swishing her habit, like an enormous crow. It was laughable now.

'Sister is still a sour old prune, probably got dementia. She's already repeated herself a few times tonight,' Dora murmured.

A woman further down the table stood and took a photo of everyone. June tossed back her wine and was pouring another.

'So are you married, Vivian?' asked Dora.

'A widow,' I replied. 'My husband died ten years ago. I have one daughter. What about yourself?'

'Oh, me,' she said, 'I'm divorced, but isn't everyone these days.'

'Any children?' I speared an olive.

'Yeah, a son. He lives with his father.'

I turned to June. 'How about you?' Are you in the single, married, or the divorced club?' She wasn't wearing any rings.

'I was married until three months ago, thought we were happy, that was until he left me for his art student. Twenty, with red hair, saw a photo of her once, it slipped out of his coat pocket. I should've suspected something. He was often working late.'

I didn't know what to say. My mouth felt dry. The art student sounded exactly like my daughter, although there were hundreds of students who could fit that description. Was it just too much of a coincidence?

June gave a loud hiccup. 'Oops, sorry.'

The sister scowled.

'You've gone quiet. Are you okay?' Dora peered at me.

'I'm fine. Sorry to hear about the break-up, June.'

She waved her hand, 'Oh, forget I mentioned it. At least we didn't have kids. He never wanted them.' She refilled her glass.

I couldn't stop thinking about the possibility of its being Francine. What if I told her that her husband's lover could be my daughter? She'd already had far too much wine.

The main course arrived, a lamb and spinach pie with small roast potatoes. I wasn't feeling very hungry.

'This is delicious. Wish I could cook as good.' Dora took a large mouthful of pie.

June picked at hers.

Dora nudged me. 'Look at that Angelique. Still thinks she's teacher's pet.'

Angelique, with a big smirk on her painted face, had her arm around Sister. I wondered about the other women. Did some still cling to their faith? I hadn't been near a church in years. I'd outgrown the institution with its dogmas and its hypocrisy.

Dora leaned back in her chair. She pulled down her skirt zipper a fraction. 'Can breathe now. Nearly wasn't going to come.'

'Why?' I remembered my own reservations.

'I'm living in Leura, got my own café, been open six months and it's doing well.'

'Good for you.' I gave her hand a gentle squeeze.

'What about you, June? Are you working?' Dora ate the last of her pie.

'I'm an editor for a publishing house. It has its ups and downs, but sure beats sitting at home on my own.' Her words were slurred. She gave another hiccup.

'So what are you doing, Viv?' Dora asked.

'I'm a dressmaker.'

'Still an expert with the old needle, huh. Do you remember when I took a year, a whole year, just to make a baby's dress?' Dora chuckled.

'And I used to have to thread the sewing machine for you when Sister wasn't looking.' I grinned.

'I know. Don't remind me.' Dora ran a hand through her hair.

Desserts had arrived, Baklava and coffees.

'I love this stuff.' Dora dived into her slice.

I dropped two sugar cubes into my coffee, then added a drop of milk. June hadn't touched the cake or the coffee. It was almost ten-thirty.

June struggled to her feet, made her garbled farewells before leaving.

'Hope she'll be all right,' I uttered to nobody in particular.

Dora handed me her business card. 'If you're ever in the area, call in for a cuppa.'

I took her card, but my thoughts were with June, who would return to isolation and a cabinet full of alcohol.

I entered the house and went straight into Francine's room. I gazed at her guitar. She'd excelled in music. A very promising student, one of her teachers had said, way back when Francine was in primary school. And now she was wasting her life with this moron. How dare he manipulate my daughter. He has not only destroyed one life, but two. Poor June hitting the bottle hard.

The phone rang. It was Francine. 'Mum, I've been so silly. He's decided to go back to his wife.' she cried.

I gripped the receiver. There was a pause. 'Can I come home?'

Hide and Seek

'You must've seen that tea set in my Aunt Ruth's glass cabinet. The cups had small yellow flowers and the saucers gold scalloped edges,' her mother said, ruffling her fine grey hair.

'No, I didn't notice a tea set when we were there,' Jasmine coughed, then looked away as she laid the table for breakfast. 'There' referred to a holiday in England thirty or more years earlier.

Jasmine couldn't follow where this statement was leading. Why all the fuss about a tea set? Why bring it up now? She was twelve, no more than thirteen at the time. Dancing to Elton John's music and writing naughty notes to the butcher's apprentice.

Her mother had been quieter than usual, ever since that telephone call early this morning, mused Jasmine.

'Everybody knew.'

'Knew what?' she snapped. Why was her mother being so vague?

For a moment, there was silence. Fickle rain tapped on the windows.

Her mother stroked the billowing curtains. 'Suppose I should've told you years ago.'

'Told me what!' Jasmine tossed her blonde hair. She briskly buttered her toast.

Her mother sighed and lit her fifth, or was it her sixth, cigarette.

Jasmine gazed out the window. It had been wet the day her father died. Her mother smoked twice as much and only left the house if she had to. Jasmine did the shopping and paid the bills. She had no close friends. Lovers, collected like spare buttons, soon vanished, once she mentioned the word commitment.

'You're better off single,' was always her mother's reply.

Was she perhaps referring to her own relationship with Jasmine's father? Their furious arguments followed by weeks of reticence.

Did Jasmine remind her mother of him – tall with blue eyes and alabaster skin?

Thunder startled them.

'I hate storms.' Her mother stubbed out her cigarette and rubbed her arms.

'What were you going to tell me?' asked Jasmine.

'What do you mean?'

Jasmine rolled her eyes, 'You started to say that everyone knew something.'

Her mother frowned, 'Storms remind me of being in the London Underground during the war. Listening to those bombs being dropped and wondering whose house had been hit. Whose lives had been destroyed. Nearly lost my little brother in the air raid shelter through whooping cough. Thought he was a goner at one stage.'

'You talk about it as if it were yesterday.' Jasmine added sugar to her coffee.

'Well, it sure feels like yesterday to me.' Her mother sat at the table, brushing at imaginary crumbs. 'You know that call I got this morning.'

'Yes, what about it?' Jasmine wasn't going to make it easy for her.

'It was my ex-husband.'

Jasmine spluttered on her coffee. 'What! What ex-husband?'

'Don't look so shocked. I was young once. Young and naïve. We met in England during the war, in an air raid shelter of all places.' She fidgeted with the lace tablecloth. 'We were in love and weeks later got married. My Aunt Ruth gave us that tea set as a wedding present. We had to leave it behind when we came to Australia.'

Jasmine swallowed. Felt numb. 'What happened?'

'Nigel had a drinking problem. It became more than just a few social drinks. I got tired of his promises to stop. We eventually divorced after five years.'

Jasmine bristled. Her mother had had this other man. Other life.

'Were there any children?' She held her breath.

'No.'

'Did Dad know?'

'Yes. But I warned him never to tell you.'

'Why?'

'Because as the years went on it just got harder to explain.'

'So why has he suddenly called?'

'Well, he'd like to see me. Told me he's off the drink. Got my number from Aunt Ruth, called in to see her when he was last in England. The truth is, Jas, I've never stopped loving him.' She wiped her eyes.

'So what am I supposed to do? Throw bouquets?'

There was a knock at the door.

'That'll be him.' Her mother patted her hair. 'Do I look all right?' She sounded like a teenager about to go on her first date.

Jasmine hopped up. Fled to her bedroom. She opened her cupboard and pulled out a music box. The key was pasted in the back of her diary. She unlocked the box and pulled out a spoon. A now very tarnished spoon. The same one stolen from that unlocked glass cabinet in Aunt Ruth's parlour yonks ago. Weird how nobody noticed it went missing. It only took seconds for Jasmine to open the door and snatch the spoon. Moments later, the adults had entered the room, lighting each other's cigarettes. Jasmine never told anyone about her kleptomania. The thrill of not getting caught still gave her a high.

She heard chatter. Bursts of laughter. Suppose I'd better make an appearance.

She pulled a face in the mirror. 'Tea set. What tea set?'

Kissing Gecko

A furnace heat engulfs us as we leave the airport. My partner, Leo, is way ahead as usual. I run a finger inside the neck of my skivvy. Sweat trickles between my breasts. Everyone else is in T-shirts, shorts and thongs. Doesn't winter ever make a guest appearance in Townsville?

'C'mon, chooky,' Leo bellows at me as he dances on the pavement.

A battered car pulls up alongside us.

'Hey, Leo.' A woman with freckles and cropped red hair leans out the window. 'Quit the dancin' and get in the car. I can't stop here, I'll get booked.'

He turns. His grin vanishes like a magician who's run out of tricks.

'G'day, I'm Janice, Leo's aunt. Your ports can't go in me boot 'cause its busted. You'll have to try and squeeze them in the back.' She eyes our suitcases.

'Did it just happen?' I can hear the tension in Leo's voice.

'Nah, it was weeks ago, but I can't afford to get it fixed. Me rent's overdue and Bob is sick again. We gotta fly to Brisi for treatment.'

'Same old Janice. Always broke.' Leo heaves the suitcases into the back of the car.

She lights a cigarette.

'You still got dosh for smokes but.' He winds down the window.

'Don't you ever give up, Leo.' Janice glances at me in the rear-view mirror.

Houses on stilts, a service station and shops rush past us.

'Like it here?' Leo asks me as he tears open a bag of marshmallows. He eats quickly.

'Don't know yet. I've only just arrived,' I reply.

'You need to go on a diet, man. You're much fatter since the last time,' says Janice.

'Huh,' he snorts, 'I was only a kid then.'

Moments later, he offers me the last marshmallow.

I shake my head. 'Where's the big banana?' I ask. Anything to lighten the mood.

'That's in Coffs, darl,' says Leo.

Janice titters. The car swerves.

'Hey, watch out!' he yells.

We drive past a shopping mall and a few golden arches. Like churches, their doctrine is everywhere.

'Not long to go now,' says Leo as we enter an industrial area. He points out the sights of concrete, tile and chemical factories. 'See that red phone box on the corner. That's where I used to ring Dad's shop from.' Leo had told me countless tales about life at his parents take-away.

'Here we are.' Janice pulls up outside a ramshackle Queenslander. 'I can let youse in now, but you'll need a set of keys cut. Mum's still in hospital, won't be out for a while yet.'

Leo's grandmother Lila had had an accident only the week before. To celebrate her eightieth, she insisted on a motorbike ride, but fell off, fracturing her pelvis and breaking her right arm.

'Why did you let Grandma do such a crazy thing?' Leo slams the door then goes around to help me remove the luggage.

'You know what she's like. You can't tell her what to do,' replies Janice.

Lila sounds like a real character, I muse.

Janice unlocks the high wrought-iron gate, then leads us beneath the house and through to a steep flight of steps. Before attempting the climb, I glance at the piles of rusted machinery, a table cluttered with girlie magazines and empty beer bottles.

'Look's like Ray's been here.' She grounds out her cigarette.

Who is Ray? I wonder. Lila's toy boy perhaps? We climb the stairs.

'Ray's my uncle. He lives here on and off. He's got a property further north with over twenty horses,' Leo tells me between puffs.

'You should do more exercise, man.' Janice throws off her thongs and unlocks the door.

'I do plenty of exercise when Kate and I go feed the ducks.'

'What ducks?' she asks.

'The ducks near my place. I live near a park,' I reply, wheeling my case through the dank hallway.

'We shoot ducks up here. Well, Ray does.' Janice gives me a smirk.

'Lovely,' I murmur, raising my eyes.

'This isn't Sydney, you know, with all those bloody do-gooders and greenies.' She flings open a door to our right. 'This is your room.'

'Oh, so we get to sleep in the same room. Bet Grandma wouldn't approve, hey.' Leo winks at me.

'Grandma ain't here and what she don't know…' Janice yawns.

Dented pillows and rumpled sheets. Had Ray or somebody else been sleeping here?

Leo catches my look of dismay. He pulls aside the tattered curtain. 'What happened to my screens? I put them on all the windows.'

'Oh, those old things. They all fell off.' She leans against the door frame, arms folded.

'Fell off, nothing! They were taken off, you mean.' Leo's face is red.

'Leo, stop your whining. That was twenty years ago. I need a smoke, just be downstairs.'

I eyed the bed, 'Looks as though…'

Leo comes over and gives me a hug. His chin rests on top of my head. 'When Janice goes, we'll hunt through the cupboards and get some fresh linen, OK.'

I nod. 'I'll change out of this skivvy, put on a T-shirt.' Before unzipping my suitcase, I slide open the wardrobe door. Stacks of dresses and jackets line the racks. 'There's no room for us to hang anything.' I know I sound petulant.

'They'll be Grandma's things,' says Leo, kicking aside a few dead cockroaches.

My stomach churns. I am afraid of cockroaches, dead or alive. I give
a sigh. 'It doesn't matter, Leo, I can get things from my case as I need
them. I only brought jeans and tops anyway.'

Janice is back. She pokes her head into the room. 'Leo, before I forget, there's some eggs in the fridge that need to be tossed, they smell a
bit funny.'

'OK, but we'll have to go out and buy stuff. Shops are too far to
walk. Can you pick us up a bit later, so we can also get a spare set of
keys cut. Tomorrow I'm going to hire a car.'

'Yeah, suppose, but after I pick up me granddaughter from school.
Say about three-thirty. See youse.' Janice goes.

Rotten eggs and an unmade bed. Janice deserves the hospitality
award of the year.

'What are you thinking about,, darl?' Leo kisses me on the neck.

I spin around. 'Didn't your family know we were coming?'

'Yeah, I told Grandma and Sharon three months ago.'

'Sharon?'

'Oh, that's Janice's older sister. She's nice. You'll like her and Uncle
Ray.'

'Yes,' I say, 'I'm sure I'd just love to meet a duck shooter and his
wife.'

'Oh, c'mon,' Leo squeezes me, 'it's not that bad and tomorrow we'll
hire a car, get out and do our own thing.'

I shrug, then moments later pull off my skivvy and jeans.

'Ah,' Leo's eyes gleam. 'Now, that's more like it.'

I back away, 'Don't you be getting any ideas.'

The phone rings.

'I bet that's Grandma now.' He races out.

As I button my brunch coat, I hear a sound like somebody kissing.
It will start, stop, then start again. I look around but can't see anything.
Is it Leo messing about? I sneak out the room and into the hallway,
press my ear against the open lounge door. Leo is talking on the phone,
so it couldn't have been him. The kissing noise starts again. Who or
what is it? I flounce into the room.

Leo grins at me. 'Yeah, Grandma, Kate's here. Do you want to have a word?' He passes me the handset.

'Hello, Lila.' I try to sound chirpy.

'Hello, Kate. Settled in yet?' She has a young voice.

'Yes, just trying to cope with this heat.'

'Oh, this is nothin'. Wait until summer, then you'll know what heat is. Can get to forty! So when are you and Leo comin' to see me?'

'Leo's hiring a car, so probably sometime tomorrow.'

'That's good, 'cause at least I'll have me hair permed. The hairdresser's comin' around today. And I might even get me nails painted.'

Eventually, I say my goodbyes and give the handset to Leo. He chats for a few more minutes, then hangs up.

I stare at the chipped ornaments on the Welsh dresser. 'Leo, when I was in the bedroom, I heard a weird noise, like kissing, but I didn't see anything.'

'Oh, that's only a gecko.' He heads towards the kitchen.

I follow. 'A what?'

'A gecko. It's a lizard, native to Queensland.'

A frying pan thick with grease lies in the sink. Ants scurry across the bench tops and windowsills.

I open the fridge door and quickly cover my nose. The smell would knock an elephant out. I reach in for the carton of eggs. 'Get rid of these.' I thrust them at Leo. I begin to sift through the other items; three avocados, a tub of butter, and a bunch of over-ripe bananas. 'I'll make us a cup of tea, if you don't mind it black.'

'Yes, fine,' replies Leo. 'I'll just go and unpack a few things.'

Rummaging through the cupboards, I find two mugs and give them a scrub. As I open the drawer to get the spoons, a huge cockroach crawls out. I scream and rush from the kitchen.

'What's up?' Leo appears.

Heart pounding, I brush past him and run to the bedroom. My voice trembles. 'There's a big cockroach in the cutlery drawer.'

'I'll get rid of it, don't worry.'

Moments later he returns, sits on the bed and slides an arm around my waist. 'It's gone. Now, how about that cuppa?'

If there is one cockroach, there'd be heaps more. I don't want to eat, drink or sleep here. Is it too late to book a flight home? But how would Leo react? Angry, disappointed? He was so keen to come and he hasn't seen his grandma in years. Two weeks. Did I have the stamina?

Leo takes hold of my hand and massages each finger. 'Not much of a welcome, is it? Grandma's been in hospital, don't forget.' He doesn't look at me.

'That's no excuse! The place is filthy and Janice can't even be bothered to throw out those putrid eggs.'

'She's always been a lazy cow. Didn't she say she'd pick us up about three-thirty? I hate relying on her, but if she's not here, I'll call her on the mobile.'

Four o'clock comes and goes.

At close to four-thirty, Leo calls Janice. 'Where the bloody hell is she? Both the house and mobile are on message bank.' He strokes his bristly chin.

'You need a shave.' I smile. 'You look like Man Friday.' I give him a peck on the cheek.

Suddenly, Leo's mobile rings. It's Janice.

'Huh, says Leo. 'Thought you weren't coming. See you outside in a minute.'

I spring from the bed. 'I'll get changed.'

The car is stifling. Janice smokes as the radio plays a disco hit from the eighties. She doesn't give us a reason for coming late. Leo, with his arms folded, mutters something about cancer. Janice turns up the volume.

She pulls up outside a hardware store. 'You can get your keys cut here.' She hands Leo the originals. 'I'll wait until you're finished, then we'll go to the mall. I'm outta smokes and gotta pay me phone bill.'

Inside the store, fans whirr overhead. While Leo deals with the key cutting, I wander around.

His voice echoes. 'My dad used to have a fish and chip shop on Mooney Street. Do you know it?' he asks the assistant. He revels in telling that story.

I come across brooms, mops and decide whether to buy any. Moments later, an arm slips around my shoulders.

'Now, don't you go buying any of that stuff.'

'Janice wouldn't know one end of a broom from the other anyway,' I say as we leave the store.

On our way to the mall, Leo says to his aunt, 'First thing tomorrow I'll see about hiring a car.'

'Good, 'cause I'm flying to Brissi in two days.'

'Lets you off the hook, doesn't it? You won't have to drive us around.'

'Bob is sick. He needs to get some tests done,' she snaps.

Leo ignores her and turns to me. 'Once we get a car, we'll go and see Grandma.'

I nod.

'Have you been in to see her?' he asks Janice.

'Not for a week.'

At least she was honest, I think, gazing out the window. The traffic is light, no car horns furiously tooting. Even pedestrians take their time.

'A week!' Leo bawls.

She retaliates with a few lame excuses. They bicker all the way to the mall.

By mid-morning the following day, Leo hires a two-door hatch. I am eager to escape from the cockroaches and the lack of clean linen.

We'd spend a week with his other Aunt Sharon at her beach house, then the remainder of our holiday at his uncle's farm at Proserpine. Did Ray read girlie magazines and drink beer all day? What kind of a marriage do he and Sharon have? It seems a strange arrangement with her at the beach house and him on his farm.

On the way to Sharon's, Leo suggests we call to the hospital and see his grandma. He points out various landmarks, 'There's... And see, that used to be a...'

Construction everywhere. Down with the old, authentic dwellings riddled with tradition, history. I begin to scratch my arms, legs and the tops of my feet.

'Stop that scratching, you'll only make it worse.'

'I must have been bitten by something.'

'Yes, me.' He gnashes his teeth.

We enter the hospital car park.

Perching on the end of the bed is Lila with her newly permed hair and her varnished nails.

'About bloody time.' She holds out one frail arm. The other is in a cast.

Leo gives her a big squeeze.

'Watch me arm,' she cries, but I can tell she loves the attention.

'Is that your grandson?' somebody sings out.

'Yeah, the oldest and the fattest one.' Lila giggles.

Leo shoves me forward. 'Gran, this is Kate.'

'Hello, darling. Leo never stops talking about you.'

I kiss her lightly on her powdered cheek.

Leo sits on a chair by the bed. 'How's the food?'

She pulls a face, 'Not much. I only have the soups and the desserts.'

'But that's not enough, Gran. You're gotta build up your strength.'

She tuts. 'I've got physio morning, noon and night. Be here for bloody weeks yet.'

I start scratching my legs again. Red lumps appear around my ankles and at the backs of my calves.

'You want to be careful you don't catch that Ross River fever. Mossies up here can be real little buggers.' Lila peers at my bites.

'Don't say that, Gran. Kate's already had a scare with the cockroaches at your place. Doesn't that Janice ever do any cleaning for you?' Leo says.

'Don't be hard on her. She's been through a lot.'

'She smokes like a chimney. Anyway, enough about her. What made you go and do such a crazy thing?

She looks at us wide-eyed. 'What are you talking about, Leo?'

'You know, riding on the back of a motorbike.'

'He wasn't going real fast and, anyway, I had to do something special for my birthday.'

'But you could've been killed.'

'Huh, I'll outlive you, my boy. Now,' she indicates her cast, 'give me your autograph.'

He draws a pineapple with a funny face.

There is a rattle of trolleys as staff deliver lunch trays.

'We'd better go, Gran.' He gives her another hug.

'Don't forget to let me know when you two are getting married.' She winks at me. 'I just love a party.'

On the way to the beach house, I tear at my skin.

'Will you stop that!' Leo slaps my thigh.

'I can't help it. You're OK, they haven't bitten you.'

'They probably don't like the taste of me.'

I pull a comb through my knotted hair, then adjust the rear-view mirror. There is a smear of dirt on my nose.

The drive to the beach house is about forty minutes from Townsville. Lucky for air conditioning. This heat is exhausting.

'What if I catch that Ross River fever?'

'You won't catch that. You don't have a temperature, do you?' He places a hand across my forehead.

I push it away. 'Watch the road!'

We drive slowly along a tree-lined street.

'There's Sharon.' Leo points to an attractive fifty-something woman who is weeding the garden.

'Hey, Sharon,' Leo leans out the window and gives the horn a loud toot.

She turns, waves, then saunters over. She gapes at our cases in the back seat. 'Thought you were staying at Mum's.'

'Kate didn't like the other guests.'

She frowns, 'What other guests?'

'The cockroaches,' I say, stepping out the car.

She laughs, 'Oh, them. They won't hurt you.'

Before I can reply, Leo says, 'C'mon, let's get our stuff inside. What's for lunch? I'm starving.'

As we drink our tea and munch our sandwiches, Sharon asks Leo how long we intend to stay.

'Oh, a week, then Kate and I will go to Prossi and stay with Uncle Ray. Take a look at his horses.'

'Bloody horses!' she explodes. 'That's all he ever thinks about. He won't come here to the beach house. Reckons he hates it.'

After lunch, Sharon shows us to our room. She thrusts a load of linen at me. 'Here, make your bed, I'm going for my walk.'

As I straighten the sheet, I say, 'I don't think Sharon is all that rapt in our being here.'

'No, she's nice, is Sharon. Has a hard time with Uncle Ray, though.'

I pull on the pillowcases, 'Doesn't sound like they see each other very much.'

'He's got a bit of a temper. Coming here gives her a break.' He bounces on the bed.

A few minutes later, the screen door slams.

'I'm back,' Sharon shouts. 'You two can stop your canoodling now.'

'That was a quick walk.' says Leo.

'It's sprinkling.' Sharon enters the room. She stares at my legs. 'Those bites look bad. I've got some cream you can use. I get bitten too.'

'Thanks. It's driving me mad.'

'See,' says Leo, patting me on the shoulder. 'I told you that Sharon is the nice one.'

'Huh, you're full of bullshit, Leo.' She leaves the room.

Sharon has a never-ending list of jobs for Leo: clearing the gutters, painting cupboards and mowing lawns. 'Got to keep him from getting bored,' she says.

Each morning and evening, we go for a walk. Before reaching the beach, we have to dart between menacing coconuts.

'If one of them hits you, you're a goner.' Sharon grins.

We increase our pace, all the while looking up.

On one of our walks, she speaks about Ray. 'He's forever ringing me. I get no peace. He wants to know when I'm coming to Proserpine. I hate it there. He's got twenty-six horses, two in foal. He's always drinking, gets abusive, tells me to pack my port and get the hell out. I'm bloody sick of it.'

I look behind us. Leo is a long way back.

'Have you ever thought of leaving him?' I look at the calm ocean. Seagulls, like white handkerchiefs, dance on the waves.

'Yeah, heaps of times, but he'll only come after me.' She bends to pick up a shell. 'Pretty, isn't it?'

I finger the shell. The delicate pink is like a baby's inner ear.

'I got married too young.' she says.

'How old were you?'

'Twenty-two.'

'But that's not so young!'

'Back then it was. Ray was ten years older. Mum hates him. Still does. He drank a bit even when we first met. Before I had the kids, I left him, but he came after me and…'

'Hey,' Leo shouts out as he runs to catch us up. 'Didn't you two hear me calling?'

'Don't say anything,' Sharon whispers.

Gasping, Leo throws himself onto the sand.

'You're too fat,' she says.

'What were you two yakking about?'

I glance at Sharon. 'Oh, just women's stuff.'

'Having a go at us blokes again, I bet.' He brushes sand from his T-shirt.

'Yeah, something like that,' I reply.

About twenty or so minutes later, 'C'mon, get up, Leo, I've gotta get home and cook tea,' says Sharon as she heads back.

'Forget about cooking. Let's have a meal at that pub near here.' Leo stands.

Sounds good to me. I am tired of washing up every night.

'It's too expensive, Leo. Anyway, I've got fish fillets and veg in the freezer.' She catches my look of disappointment.

'She's right, the pub would probably cost us an arm and a leg.' He places an arm around my shoulders.

'But we're on holiday, Leo.' I feel like a child who is refused an ice cream.

'Yeah, I know,' he sighs then gives me a big kiss on the lips.

'No canoodling, you two.' Sharon titters.

'Canoodling!' I murmur, what does she think we are – teenagers?

On our last night with Sharon, she makes a spaghetti bolognese. Every few minutes, her mobile rings.

'Aren't you going to answer it?' I ask. My head is feeling woolly. I didn't have that much wine.

'No, it'll only be Ray wanting to know when I'm coming to Prossi.'

Leo grins as he pours himself a Coke. I finish my meal and sit back in the chair, but still feel strange, light-headed.

Leo pats me on the arm. 'Are you all right?'

'Yes, why?' I swallow.

'You've just gone a bit pale,' Sharon says as she clears the table.

Pushing back my chair, I stand, then slowly make my way out of the kitchen and into the hall. As I am about to enter the bathroom, a miasma of darkness descends.

Seconds later, I am on the floor. I open my eyes and look up into Leo's anxious face.

'What are you doing down there?' He squats beside me.

'What do you think I'm doing?' I bark. 'A new form of yoga!'

'What happened?' Sharon hovers behind him, dishcloth in hand.

'You look like a ghost,' says Leo. He turns to his aunt. 'Get her some water and make it a large glass.' He helps me into a sitting position.

The back of my head is sore. I rub it gently. 'I must've banged it on the wall when I fainted.'

Leo scrutinises the wall. 'Yes, there's a big dent in it.'

'Is there?' I turn, then notice his smile.

Sharon hands me the water. 'You've had too much wine.'

'I only had two glasses.' I sip the water greedily.

Leo wraps his arms around me and helps to lift me up.

I burst into laughter. 'I feel so silly. Before I passed out, I began to feel woozy, but I didn't want to say anything. Make a fuss.'

He hugs me. 'It's the heat. You're not used to it.'

'Now, which of you is going to wipe up? I've got to make a few calls,' says Sharon.

Days later, whenever we talk about my fainting episode, we often chuckle. Sharon doesn't see the funny side, though – I bet she still thinks we blame her cooking.

Proserpine is a three-hour drive from Sharon's. The undulating land-scape is not so enticing, as we come across dead possums and wallabies. An occasional antique shop and garden centre interrupt the monotony.

Leo pinches my arm.

'Ouch! That hurt.'

'Prossi isn't far now. You can have a ride on one of Uncle Ray's horses.'

'What! Are you kidding? No way. I can't ride a horse.'

'There's nothing to it. I'm going to have a go. Uncle Ray will be mad if you don't.'

'The answer is no, Leo.' I fold my arms and stare ahead.

An hour or so later, we drive into Ray's property. Surrounded by trucks and a few horse floats is a two-storey house with flaking paint and no flyscreens.

'Anyone home?' Leo calls out the car window.

A barking Dobermann bounds up to the car.

'Hello, boy.' Leo opens the door.

I am more apprehensive.

'C'mon, Kate,' says Leo as he pats the dog. 'He won't bite you.'

I undo my seatbelt and slowly, very slowly, open the door. The Do-bermann comes over and sniffs my hand.

A male voice booms, 'Hey, Leo, ya bastard!' A man in his sixties, barefoot, of medium height approaches us. He pumps Leo's hand then takes a gulp of his beer. 'Who's this?'

Leo makes the introductions. The Dobermann goes over to one of the trucks and lifts his leg.

'How long are youse stayin'?' He reeks of sweat and alcohol.

'A week, then we fly home.' Leo kicks at the turf.

Ray rubs his bleary eyes, 'Wanna beer?' he asks me.

'No thanks, but I'd love a cup of tea.'

'Tea, huh!' he sneers. 'Don't ya drink?'

'Yes, a glass or two with meals, but…' I glance at my watch. 'It isn't even ten o'clock.'

He jerks his head. 'OK, suit yaself. What about you, Leo?'

'I'll have a Coke.'

I swat at the fierce horseflies as we head towards the house. In the kitchen, spilt beer, newspapers and unopened business letters litter the table.

Ray fills the kettle. 'Make yourselves at home.' He opens a cupboard and pulls out a mug. 'Tea bag all right?'

'Yes.' I sit down.

A fly settles on the beer.

While the kettle boils, Ray opens the door, 'Gotta see to me horses. Wanna come?'

Leo snatches a Coke from the fridge and follows his uncle.

Ray pops his head back through the door. 'Your room is at the end of the corridor.'

I finish my tea, then take a walk around the living room. Photos of a younger Ray and his horses are everywhere. There is only one photo of Sharon and their two adult children. I open the bedroom door. A woman's clothes are strewn across a rumpled bed. I am getting used to this northern kind of hospitality.

I open the window and let some air into the stuffy room. I look out to see Ray placing a saddle across one of his horses. Leo strokes its mane.

He glances up. 'Come down. Ray's got the horse ready for you.'

I shake my head. 'No, I'm happy to watch you instead.' I lean on the sill.

'C'mon, it could be the only chance you ever get,' he insists.

Ray whispers something to him. Moments later, Leo puts on a helmet and boots. I stifle a giggle as Leo makes numerous attempts to get onto the horse.

Ray places a plastic chair next to the animal. 'Now try.'

Leo gets one leg onto the chair then heaves himself over the horse's back with the other leg. He is upright in the saddle, except the chair is still entangled in his left foot.

The more Leo tries to shake off the chair, the more anxious the horse becomes. I hold my breath.

'Don't panic,' Ray snarls, as he gets rid of the chair, takes hold of the bridle and leads them away.

That night, sausages and baked beans are on the menu. Our evening's entertainment is listening to Ray's drunken rambles about Sharon and his mother-in-law.

The next morning, after much persuasion by Leo, I pluck up the courage to have a ride. In spite of my decision, I delay the event by making extra toast and eating as slowly as I can.

'Hurry up, Ray's waiting.' Leo whips up my cup and plate.

'But I haven't finished yet,' I splutter on a mouthful of toast.

'You have now.' He grins. 'You'll love it, Kate. The horses are beautiful, even if I am a bit sore today.' He rubs his backside.

Ray heaves the saddle onto what looks like the largest of his horses.

'He's enormous.' My voice quivers. I lightly pat his forehead.

'Nah, I've got bigger ones than him.' He tightens the bridle.

The horse nods and snorts.

'What's his name?'

'Rudolph.'

Is this a joke?

Leo hands me a helmet and boots. 'Now, one foot in the stirrup, then swing your other leg over his back. 'We've got hold of him, don't worry.'

I place my foot as he instructs into the stirrup and as I swing my leg across the saddle, Ray mutters, 'Just pretend you're throwing that leg over Leo.'

He roars with laughter, the horse rears and I fall onto the ground.

Leo helps me up and encourages me to try again.

'No.' I glare at Ray before walking off.

For a few days, I have a bruised bottom and an even bigger bruised ego.

Only a short time left before I return to clean linen, sanity and people who don't use words like ay, or hey. I have no more books to read or cards to write. The town, even though in easy walking distance, only has two pubs, a supermarket and a post office

On the veranda, I recline in the chair, close my eyes and listen to the geckos. The phone rings, Leo answers it. Soon after, he rushes out,

'Guess what! Grandma's signed herself out of hospital. She's at home. I'll have to cancel our flight. We'll go there first thing tomorrow.'

'But…'

'Huh, thought you were rid of us, didn't ya. Ray takes a swig of beer. 'You might even get to kiss one now that you and Leo have gotta stay longer.'

'Kiss what?'

'A gecko.'

Bitchy Business

I lightly run my finger across the designs of apples, blueberries and lemons on the drinking glass. My friend Trini had bought six of them for my fiftieth. I filled the glass with water, took a sip and closed my eyes.

Hours before Trini and Zoula's arrival, I set about organising their sleeping arrangements. My plan is for us to attend a house auction, then take a gander at my local farmers' market. For dinner, I make a vegetarian quiche and a couscous salad. Do I really look forward to this girls' weekend? To be honest, Trini and Zoula can be a pain at times, but it might do me good to relax with a glass of wine and a shared cigar. Trini and I have been performing this ritual for years.

I make up the bed in the spare room. Trini will be better in here, while Zoula, weighing no more than fifty kilos, could sleep comfortably on my sixties sofa. After making the bed, I open my wardrobe door. Zoula's denim skirt, a blouse and a cardigan are hanging next to two of my coats. I open one of the drawers. Inside, neatly folded is her nightie, stack of paper towels and a bikini. Bikini! I almost give a giggle. I never saw her wearing that before. She is always covered from head to toe, whenever we go to the beach. A rarity nowadays. I frown. There is far too much of her stuff here. It looks as if she'd gradually been bringing more clothes over.

Once, when I reproached her, she tells me that it is too much of a hassle carrying things back and forth on public transport. She stays with me at Christmas, Easter and some weekends. At the time, I relented. Leaving a few things at my place is no harm, I suppose. I did feel empathy for Zoula. Her days are spent visiting her ninety-year-old mother in a nursing home. Zoula's social life revolves around the dramas with staff and patients.

I rifle through clothes and hangers. Soon I won't have any room left for my own stuff. Zoula and I need to have a serious heart to heart.

'She hasn't got a life,' Trini comments on one or two occasions.

But what did having a life mean exactly? Trini's husband is married to his bagpipes. Most of his weekends are spent with fellow band members in the Southern Highlands.

'I hardly ever see him,' Trini often whinges. 'And when he is home, he's either practising on those bloody pipes or doing his headstands.'

I stop rifling and shut the wardrobe door. They'll be here soon.

Zoula arrives first with several plastic bags and a flushed face. Menopause madness, or overdosing on vitamin D? Dumping the bags on the table, she rushes over to my sink. A few moments and a dripping face later, she pulls out a pile of paper towels.

'Here, take some.' She quickly pats her face.

I refuse, musing on the pile in the drawer.

'Is Trini still coming?' she asks, handing me a container of home-made Greek biscuits.

'Yes, a bit later. Hope she can make it for dinner.' I roll my eyes, losing count of the times she was an hour or two late.

Over coffee, Zoula talks about the latest episode in the nursing home. 'A naked man was found inside my mother's room.'

I laugh. 'What! Bet your mum got a shock, or maybe she enjoyed it.'

'My mother was asleep, and anyway she's got dementia.'

Zoula doesn't have much to be humorous about. Her mother's health deteriorating and a bunch of greedy relatives eager to get their hands on the family home.

The doorbell chimes.

'That'll be Trini.' I glance at the kitchen clock. 'She's early for once.'

Zoula nods as she refolds the paper napkins.

'Hi.' Trini pecks me on both cheeks. She trips on the front step.

I steady her. Trini never fails to make an entrance. I lead her into the dining room.

Zoula is bending over the sink again. Cold tap on full bore. She splashes her face several times, then heads across to Trini. I turn off the tap.

'Oh, how lovely to see you,' Zoula cries.

They hug briefly.

Trini then slumps into a chair. 'My blood pressure must be sky high,' she says.

'Oh, and why would that be?' I ask, filling the kettle.

Zoula urges Trini to take a paper towel. She refuses.

'These stupid drivers blasting their horns at me. They don't know how to drive.'

I refrain from replying that they can't be crazier than you going through stop signs. After one or two of these episodes, I made sure that I don't go too far in the car with her.

'Tea, everyone.' I hold up my new green pot.

Trini nods.

Zoula insists on an iced coffee. 'That's if you have any ice cream.'

'Yes, I bought a new one yesterday.' I open the freezer.

Trini scrabbles inside her bag, then hands me a box of chocolate almonds. 'I had to hide these from Henry. He eats everything in sight. The other day I found a half-eaten bag of marshmallows hidden inside his rolled-up kilt.'

Later after dinner and drinks, Trini and I pass the cigar back and forth.

'Just like the old days, huh,' she grins. 'Henry is up for sale. Any takers?' She kicks off her sandals.

Zoula grunts. She considers all men bastards, ever since her husband abandoned her years ago for a wealthy cheese-maker.

I am currently celibate. My last fling, ten years my junior, was a pill-popping skateboard rider. After months of rows and a black eye, I'd had a gutful.

The next morning, I am up extra early. I call both Zoula and Trini before I organise the breakfasts.

At eight o'clock, Zoula appears. 'Where's Trini?' she asks as she pats her wet face with a paper towel.

'She should be up by now.' I reply, going up the hallway and pinning my ear to the door.

No sound. I knock. Still no sound. I then open the door. A mound of bedclothes twitch. A tousled head appears.

She gives a big yawn. 'Oh, what's the time?'

'Time to get up. I called you before. Didn't you hear me?'

She pulls the doona back over her head.

'We've got the market on today and that auction.' I stand by the bed, feet apart, hands on hips.

She mutters something. Her voice is muffled.

'What was that?' I ask.

'I took half a sleeping tablet last night.'

No wonder she is so groggy. But why take a tablet when she knew that we'd organised the market and the auction?

'C'mon, get ready, we're going to start breakfast.' I leave the room.

Zoula pours herself an orange juice.

I sit down. 'We may as well start, Trini's still in bed.'

'Still in bed! My God. But she knew we were going out.'

I nod, getting up to place two slices of bread into the toaster. 'Apparently she took a sleeping tablet last night.'

'Oh, no,' Zoula shakes her head. 'We're going to miss the day.'

About half an hour or so later, Trini totters to the table. She ruffles her hair and gives a stretch. 'Oh, so I see you're finally using my glasses.'

I pour her a juice. 'To friendship.'

We raise our glasses.

Zoula eyes their designs of fruit. 'They look very good quality, must've been expensive.'

Trini gives a sniff. 'Well, it was for a special birthday.' She pats my hand.

I glance at the wall clock. 'The market will be open now. All the best stuff goes early.'

'Oh, we'll make it, don't worry.' Trini pours milk onto her cereal. 'I forgot to bring my vitamins, can we go past a chemist first?'

I raise my eyes.

'And I'll need to wash my hair, it's too oily.'

I make my way to the sink, clatter the dishes and squeeze liquid over them. Due to Trini's ineptitude, we would miss not only the market, but the auction too.

Zoula heads out of the dining room, tells us she is going to brush her teeth and give her face another splash.

'I think we'll leave the market for another time.' I say, trying to keep the molten lava out of my voice. 'Let's just concentrate on the auction this afternoon, shall we?'

Trini wipes the sleep out of her eyes. 'OK, that'll give me more time to wash my hair and get those vitamins.'

I clatter more dishes. She had no intention of going. Once I finish the washing up, I turn round. Trini avoids eye contact as she finishes her coffee. I head to my room to put on some make-up. I take my time. Deliberately. I needn't have risen so early.

I examine the pimple on my chin, then camouflage it with concealer. After outlining my eyes with khol and adding a little mascara, I return to the dining room. Trini is still sitting at the table. I can hear Zoula splashing in the bathroom.

'She's very devious, you know.' Trini fidgets with the sugar bowl lid.

'Who?' I frown.

'Zoula.' she hisses.

'Zoula?' I repeat. Stare at Trini. 'What do you mean?'

'I just saw her sneak out here and put boiling water from the kettle into the glass.'

'What! No, you must be mistaken. She wouldn't do such a thing. Anybody knows that it can and will crack the glass.'

'Exactly!' Trini is wide awake now. 'And,' she runs her finger along the edge of the table, 'I bet she's shoving those paper towels down your toilet too. You really need to talk to her.'

'But she's always brought those paper towels here and when she's used them, she dries them on my small laundry line then uses them again.'

'Yuck!' Trini screws up her face.

We hear footsteps approach.

Trini hops up. 'I'd better go and have my shower, otherwise we'll never get out.'

This whole situation is crazy. Boiling water being poured into my good glasses and paper towels supposedly shoved down my toilet. But for what purpose? And did Trini really see Zoula trying to destroy my glasses? Maybe she imagined it. After all, Trini was in zombie land with that sleeping tablet, even though she claimed it was only a half one. And anyway, why would Zoula want to jeopardise our friendship? Jealousy perhaps? Is she envious of my home? My life? She does have her own unit. Her hard-drinking next-door neighbours keep her awake most nights with their loud sex romps. She often talks about selling, but she hasn't made any effort to look for another place.

Zoula re-enters the dining room. She pushes a slide into her dark wiry hair.

'Zoula,' I say.

'Yes,' she turns.

'Um, oh nothing.' I bite my lip.

She continues out into the laundry and pegs two of the paper towels onto my line. I hide a smile, recalling Trini's screwed-up face. There is a pile of towels still on the kitchen table. I wonder, would Zoula dare to use them in my toilet? Surely she'd realise they'd block the systern. Even a child knows that.

'Where's Trini? Gone back to bed?' asks Zoula as she zips up her very tight denim skirt.

'No, she's getting ready.'

Why does Zoula insist on squeezing into a size ten when she is clearly a twelve, I think. And she needs a haircut. She never went to a hairdresser, nor a beautician for that matter. Her frugal behaviour landed her in strife more than once. I was with her recently when she began to paint all her nails from a sample bottle of varnish. The proprietor bustled over and shouted, 'It's only to be tested on one nail, not the lot!' Zoula admired her nails and answered, 'Oh, I'm sorry, I didn't know.' I fled the shop, my face burning.

Then there were the times when she'd snatch sugar sachets from cafés. 'For my unit' was her reply when I rebuked her once. And only on the odd occasion did she ever buy a coffee. I give a sigh. Am I being too harsh? Too judgemental?

'Penny for them.'

'What?' I blink.

'Your thoughts. You were miles away.' Trini clicks her fingers.

'I'm ready. Like my shoes?'

Zoula and I look down at her blue stilettos.

'They match my dress.' She gives a twirl.

She certainly has style, sophistication, when she bothers to make an effort, I think.

'Meeting a hunk at the auction, are we?' I grin.

'Oh, you never know.' She winks. 'I'm getting sick of Henry. Might just push him down the stairs one of these days. I gave him a kick recently.'

Zoula draws in her breath.

I swallow. 'Whatever for?'

'He refuses to cut the lawns and he never helps around the house. I end up doing everything.'

The situation between Trini and Henry is far worse than I imagine.

'But he seems a very good man,' says Zoula.

'Huh, you can have him. Anyway, I thought you said all men were bastards,' Trini snaps, adjusting the belt on her dress. 'C'mon, aren't we going? We'll call to a chemist on the way.'

We arrive at least fifteen minutes before the auction. None of the usual crowds milling about. Trini pulls up with a jerk outside the house. There is a sign on the gate. 'Sold'.

I crane my neck and stare at the sign. 'Oh, I can't believe it. Sold already and it didn't even go to auction.'

'That can happen. I'll ring the agent.' After a few moments on her mobile, she turns to me. 'It was sold yesterday. A private sale apparently.'

I fold my arms. First we miss out on the market and now this. 'No use hanging about then. I need a strong drink.'

We head to a local club.

'May as well have an early dinner. The bistro will be open soon,' I hint.

'I'm full from the breakfast,' Zoula sings out from the back of the car.

'That was ages ago. I'm hungry,' Trini snaps as she squeals round a corner.

A stop sign approaches. She drives straight through. I shut my eyes. I doubt that Zoula notices. She is busy making all kings of excuses as to why she's not keen on the club idea.

'You don't have to eat.' Trini glares at her in the rear-view mirror, before slamming on the brakes.

A man in a tweed cap and baggy trousers shuffles across at the lights. He holds up two fingers at us.

'Manners!' Trini pulls out her tongue at him.

'Well, you almost ran him over,' I shout, clutching onto the seat belt.

Glad to see the club in the distance. Zoula is still rattling off her excuses.

Trini and I study the menus, then both decide on the lasagne with chips.

Zoula wanders to the bar to get a glass of water. We idly chat about the club's new décor, while I observe the nose picker at the next table.

'Have you told her yet?' Trini leans across the table.

'Told her what?' I sip my brandy and Coke.

She clears her throat. 'About the hot water she poured into the glass,' she firmly reminds me, stirring her cup of tea.

'I will. Just haven't had a chance yet.'

She raises an eyebrow. 'She's such a tight arse.'

'No more than you,' I reply, getting weary of this bitching.

'What do you mean?' Her mouth hangs open.

'The time in Melbourne when we agreed to go halves with that coconut cake and I ended up paying for the lot.'

'Oh, that's because it was stale. And I didn't like the waiter. He was too arrogant.' She pulls a small mirror out of her bag and begins to apply a lipstick.

'That waiter must've thought you were drunk when you nearly fell off the stool.'

She sighs, fluffs out her collar-length hair. 'I need to get my streaks done again.'

Zoula, her face dripping, returns to the table. 'I feel very hot.' She fans herself with a coaster.

'You were a long time,' I retort.

'Oh, I had to go into the ladies. My face needs water.'

'Aren't you going to order a snack or something?' Trini sounds churlish.

Zoula shakes her head. 'I'm full. We could've eaten at your place. Why spend the money here? I'm not a person for clubs.'

'Well, the majority rules,' Trini bites.

I am still irritated by our earlier conversation and don't bother to remind Trini about another embarrassing episode in Melbourne, when she insisted there was a hair in her dinner. I was sitting next to her and could see that it was a mushroom strand. She made such a fuss the restaurant owner ended up refunding her the money.

Our meals arrive.

'You know, he could've made us wash a load of dishes, or worse still call the police,' I harp.

'Who?' Trini adds salt to her meal.

I offer Zoula a chip. She takes several.

'That waiter back in Melbourne.'

'Oh, you're not still on about him, are you? Look, that bloody cake was stale. OK!'

'Stale or not, you still should've coughed up your half.' I raise my voice.

Trini suddenly dives into her bag and throws some coins on the table. 'Here. Satisfied now?'

Heads swivel in our direction.

Zoula covers her ears. 'Please, girls, don't fight.'

Trini pushes her plate aside. She has left most of the lasagne. Another hair, I muse.

The nose picker is gone.

I glance at my watch. 'Think we'll make a move.' A duo in red shirts are setting up their equipment in the far corner. 'I'm not in the mood.'

'I'll go home once I collect my things.' Trini rises from the chair.

'Fine,' I reply.

Zoula asks me if she can stay on an extra night. I agree. I still need to talk to her about the glass incident and the amount of clothing she is leaving at my place. Does she realise that she is crossing boundaries? How can I broach the subject, mention the glass bit first, or bring up the clothes, then tell her what Trini saw? Or thinks she saw. Zoula is likely to take offence, but I have to say something. The longer I wait, the harder it will get. And if I don't speak up, Trini is mad enough to do it for me.

I quickly finish my drink.

Back at the house, Trini shoves clothes into her suitcase. She gives both Zoula and me a brief hug then leaves.

'Why is she in such a hurry?' Zoula pats her wet face with a paper towel. 'She could've stayed until tomorrow. Wasn't that the idea?'

I switch on the kettle. 'Oh, she's probably worried about Henry.' I unscrew the lid from the coffee jar.

'Henry! She wanted to push him down the stairs.' Zoula takes a bobby pin from her hair.

'Oh, I think she was just exaggerating. You know Trini, anything for attention.'

Zoula heads over to my sink. I watch closely as she pours herself a glass of water. I must speak to her about the other matters. But how to begin?

She returns to the table. 'Anything wrong?'

'No, nothing wrong. Why should there be?'

The kettle is boiled and I make our coffees. We talk for another hour or so about one of her acquaintances, who has signed all her properties over to her only son. Once the legalities were dealt with, he threw his mother out of the house. She has been sleeping on friends' couches ever since.

'What a stupid lady.' Zoula blows on her coffee. 'And now she wants me to let her stay in my unit.'

'What did you say?' I was curious.

'I told her no, of course. She says I could never understand her situation because I'm not a mother.'

'But that's just ludicrous. And now she hasn't even got a roof over her head. So much for families. There're overrated.'

She yawns. It is getting late. No time to go into lengthy discussions now. I rinse the cups. Tomorrow morning, I'll raise the subject during breakfast.

While Zoula showers, I prepare poached eggs and porridge. In between a wrong number and a church stalker at my door, Trini phones,

'Have you said anything to Zoula yet?' Her voice is crisp.

'No, not yet. I'm waiting for the right moment.'

'Right moment! They were very expensive glasses and…'

'All right, all right. I'm going to speak to her this morning. OK?'

'She did it. I know what I saw.' She hangs up.

Zoula appears, drying tendrils of damp hair. 'Who was on the phone?'

'Trini,' I reply, studying Zoula's face. Did she overhear the conversation?

'How is she? Has she killed Henry yet?' She smirks.

'It's not funny.' I dish out breakfast. Halfway through my porridge, I break into a babble. 'Trini claims she saw you pouring boiling water from the kettle straight into one of my glasses yesterday.' At last it was out.

Zoula's fork full of egg halts in mid-air. 'What! I never did. First, I put some cold into the glass then I added a little from the kettle. Why is she saying that's what I did?'

'Yes, and you know that boiling or even very hot water can break the glass. They were a present from Trini.'

'I know that it can crack the glass. I'm not stupid!' She continues to eat.

'I wasn't in the room at the time, so I can only go on what Trini tells me.' I push aside my bowl.

'And you believe her! After all the years we've been friends?' Zoula waves her fork at me.

'Frankly, I don't know who or what to believe. The whole weekend's been spoilt.'

'No, it hasn't. I've enjoyed your company.' Zoula places a hand on my arm. 'I love staying here.'

I nod. Should I mention her clothes now? It is the perfect opportunity.

The phone rings again. It's Trini. 'Have you asked her yet?'

Sounds like someone in the background is moaning. Has she thrown Henry down the stairs? I daren't ask.

'Yes.'

'And what did she say?'

'She denied it.'

'Huh. Knew she would.' Trini slams down the receiver.

I return to the dining room.

'Who was that?' Zoula is thickly spreading butter onto her toast.

Moments later, she digs the knife into the marmalade.

'Wrong number.' I decide not to mention the clothes. I shall try to make more room in my spare wardrobe. Maybe I can hang some of her stuff on the hook behind the guest room door, or better still put it in carrier bags under the bed. Zoula takes the plates across to the sink. I give the table a brisk wipe.

'I'll get my things together. I've left another skirt here, it's the one with the buttons. Good to use around the house whenever I stay.'

I gnash my teeth.

'Is that all right?'

'Yes, of course it is.' I avoid her gaze.

'You treat me better than my sister.' She gives me a peck on each cheek before leaving.

Next day, I do the washing. As it's nearing its cycle completion, I notice soap suds erupting over my outside drain. Unusual. Soon after, I have trouble flushing my toilet. Are the two connected? I call a plumber without delay. He arrives in under an hour. He is young with a tatooed forehead and a lip stud. I explain the situation and he goes ahead with the eel and camera rigmarole. There is a blockage. Could be tree roots strangling my sewerage pipe. We sort out a quote.

He starts the following day. After what seems like hours of digging, he asks me to come outside. He is looking embarrassed. 'I've found the cause of your problem. A bunch of paper towels.'

'Paper towels!' I yell at him.

'Yes. They clump, not like toilet paper.'

'I know that. But I didn't put them down there.' I feel like a fool.

'Well, somebody did. Are you the only occupant?'

'Yes.'

'So how did they get there then?'

'How should I know?' I snap. I think for a moment or two. 'I've just remembered something. I do have a friend who stays with me now and then. She brings some paper towels over. But she wouldn't have put them down there, surely.'

'I suggest you ask her. C'mon, take a look.'

We walk over to the huge trench and I peer inside. To my horror, there is a pile of sodden towels.

'You're looking at least two grand for me to put a new pipe in and clear this all up.'

I agree to the work and the cost. It will take two days, if not three.

My thoughts torpedo. Did Zoula knowlingly flush those towels down my system? She must know they aren't biodegradable. But why do it in the first place? Stupidity? Vindictiveness? It seems that Trini is right after all. I should send Zoula the bill. How dare she damage my plumbing and think that she could get away with it. So childish, not unlike the pouring of boiling water into my drinking glass. The strange thing is, she had been bringing those towels to my place for years and I'd never had a blockage before.

I pace up and down my hallway. I stop suddenly. She did it because she is jealous of Trini. She resents being put on my sofa, while Trini has the bedroom. Yes, that's what it is. Pure envy. Did she think she wouldn't get found out? Who else uses or brings over those paper towels other than Zoula? Two grand to clean up her dirty work. My head pounds.

I pour myself a brandy. I am mortified. What a mean, horrible thing to do. We've been friends for so long. Twenty-five years, in fact. I trusted her. We have shared secrets about past lovers and I confided in her about my fear of growing old.

I need to call Zoula straight away and demand answers, or better still wait until I calm down. I should have listened to Trini. She did warn me about Zoula's sneakiness.

I want to rip her clothes to shreds. Or better still rip her to shreds. Hire a hit man.

I pour another brandy, then ring Trini. 'You were so right,' I say.

'Ah, you've seen the light about the glass.'

'Worse than that. I had to call a plumber because I had a blockage.'

'And…'

'When he dug the trench, there was a pile of paper towels at the bottom. He even had trouble getting the eel to go through.'

'What! Oh no. See, I told you. Not only did she nearly break those good glasses, but now she's stuffed up your plumbing. What a bitch.'

'Two grand it will cost me.'

'Get her to pay for it.'

'But how? I've got no proof that she did it. I didn't see her put the towels down my loo.'

'Oh, c'mon, she's the only one who brings them over. You'll have to tell her. Anyway, I'd get rid of her.'

I realise now Trini is right. She knows what Zoula is up to. She hinted as much earlier on. I've been too naïve.

'Do you know of a hit man?' I ask.

'Huh, wish I did. I need one for Henry.'

'Oh, how is he by the way?'

'He's OK, except for a sprained ankle. He took a tumble down the stairs the other night. Thinks I pushed him. He's becoming paranoid.'

Is she really trying to bump him off? 'Look, I'd better call Zoula soon and sort this mess out.'

'Good luck,' says Trini.

Before calling Zoula, I have another brandy. I take three deep breaths and dial Zoula's number.

On the fourth ring, she answers. 'Hello.' Her voice is faint.

'It's me.'

'Oh, hello, lovely to hear from you. I didn't expect a call so soon.' Her voice now is louder.

I am better to lead up to this, so we chat about a few trivial matters first.

I clear my throat, then swallow. 'While I was doing some washing, I noticed a blockage with my outside drain…' I pause.

No response.

'Anyway, I ended up calling a plumber and after he did a lot of digging, guess what he found?'

'What?' she asks.

I clench my fist. 'A load of paper towels.'

'Paper towels!' she cries.

'Yes, didn't you hear me the first time?' My head is about to detonate. 'So what do you have to say? Or rather tell me?'

'About what? I can't understand you.' Her voice goes faint again.

'Well, I'll make my point clearer, shall I? Did you at anytime flush paper towels down my loo?'

'No, of course not. How could you say such a thing?'

'So how in hell did they get there then?'

'I don't know.'

'Ha! You don't know.' My voice rises. 'But you're the one who always uses them, you bring stacks of them to my place. And you have the audacity to tell me you don't know.' I am in full throttle now, like a prosecutor who is close to winning her case.

'I swear to you, I've no idea how they got there. Truly.'

'They are not biodegradable and of course they caused a blockage.'

'I only use them to wipe my face because of my hot flushes, then I hang them on your laundry line to dry, I've always done that.'

'Well, I certainly didn't put them down there and Trini doesn't even use them, nor does she bring any over. Don't lie to me, Zoula.'

'I'm not lying to you.'

There is more bickering to and fro, but I'm not getting anywhere. She refuses to admit the damage.

'I should make you pay. Send you the bill.'

Zoula of course keeps denying it.

'Look,' I calm down a little, 'we aren't solving anything, so tomorrow if you're home I'm going to bring all your things over. I don't want anything to be left in my place ever again.' I emphasise the *ever*. This surely will get her talking. Now she will have to admit to her nasty deed.

'Yes, come tomorrow. I'll be home.'

We arrange a time, then I hang up.

I fume, but decide not to have another brandy. The end of a friendship: our twilight picnics at the beach with Zoula scouring the sand for any forgotten towels. My reaction was to warn her against dengue fever, the plague even, but Zoula being Zoula ignored this and her response was 'But I'll wash it. Towels are expensive to buy.'

I pull out her gear from the wardrobe drawers and bag it.

She is sitting on the brick fence outside her unit block when I arrive.

We exchange cool greetings and I hand her the three bags of clothing. Zoula invites me in for a coffee. I refuse.

'I never did it, you know.' She sniffs, then blows her nose.

I glare at her. 'Zoula, there's nobody else it could've been. So do you have anything else to say?'

She hangs her head. 'No.'

I turn away, walk up the street and before I cross the road, glance back. She is still sitting on the brick fence, bags at her feet.

That evening, I call Trini. I tell her about Zoula's persistent denial and my returning all of her stuff.

'Oh, forget about her. She's got plenty of her own cronies. You can have a good time without her and, besides, you'll have more room in your wardrobe now.'

Strange, how Trini so readily dismisses my long association with Zoula.

All blame was automatically laid at Zoula's door. Isn't it often the one you least suspect? I never questioned Trini about the incident.

'How about you come over to my place next week? I'll make us dinner and if it gets too late, you can stay over. We'll have the house to ourselves. Henry's had to go into hospital. Clumsy man, he ended up tripping down the back steps, broke his arm.'

'Poor Henry.' I then decide to question her about the paper towels.

'Trini. I need to ask you something.'

'Yeah, sure.'

'There's is no other way to say this.' Seconds tick. 'Did you put those paper towels down my loo?'

'What!' she yells.

I move the receiver away from my ear.

'Are you crazy? We both know it was Zoula.'

'But that's just it. I'm blaming her, but I never saw her do it.'

'She always brings those rotten paper towels to your place. You told me that yourself. You're only lucky that she hasn't done it sooner.'

'Just because she brings those towels, doesn't mean she blocked my toilet with them.'

'Oh, so you're accusing me now!'

'I'm not accusing you, Trini, I'm only asking you a question.'

'I can't believe you'd even dare to ask me.'

'Trini, there were two of you in my house and I certainly didn't stuff up my own plumbing. And another thing, how do I know that Zoula even poured boiling water into my glass? I've only got your word for it.'

'Are you calling me a liar now?' Her tone is waspish.

'No, but…'

'She's nothing but a tight-arse cow.'

'That's beside the point,' I snap.

'Believe what you like. You're a devil for punishment.' She hangs up.

I laugh out loud. Do a funny dance. My plan works.

It actually works. I got rid of the bitches at last. No more Zoula with her clothes filling up my cupboards and her tight-arse behaviour. No more Trini driving through stop signs and whingeing about Henry. What's a few grand for plumbing when I've won my freedom. The sewerage pipes are old and would've needed replacing one day. I pour another brandy.

The Bolt-hole

Comet couldn't believe his luck when he'd discovered a piece of ham at the end of his garden. He snatched and swallowed. But this time was different. Very different. Comet had not long digested the ham when his eyes bulged. He then went into a sudden convulsion, before vomiting. His recent kidney trouble stopped him from eating anything other than his special bland diet. He couldn't eat this. He couldn't eat that. It was such a bore. The ham had been delicious. He felt guilty, but it was too late now.

Comet was very fond of the Websters, who lived next door. Once he overheard them saying, 'Oh, but isn't he so thin? That diet isn't nutritious enough.'

Comet was a nervous cat and would even run from dragonflies and he couldn't stand that bossy magpie. Comet lived with Kiki. He wished he could be more like her. She never let anyone or anything worry her and she would glare and spit at any stranger foolish enough to enter the garden via the bolt-hole. This hole, a small opening halfway along the fence, was a blessing for the cats. The Websters had given their owners, Jo and Sam, permission for the bolt-hole. Comet and Kiki had access to their neighbours' garden whenever they liked. Comet had found it hard jumping the fence ever since his illness and Kiki had arthritis in her hip.

Both cats enjoyed lazing in the Websters' garden, where the strains of classical music could be heard through the open French windows. They liked listening to their neighbours, who never fought and always spoke in soft tones.

Why couldn't life with Jo and Sam be more idyllic, pondered

Comet. Why did they have to fight all the time? Why weren't they more like the Websters? Jo, the more boisterous of the two, never wore anything other than shorts and singlets. When she wasn't arguing with Sam, she'd be guzzling a bottle of beer. Sam favoured pant suits and bowler hats. She thought herself a great artist, spending hours working on her studies of nude women. Comet and Kiki were embarrassed by her paintings and longed to move into the Websters' for good.

Comet dreaded weekends when Jo, with a bellyful of beer, would taunt Sam about her paintings. Everything from crockery and bottles were slung at each other. This was the time when Comet and Kiki made their escape through the bolt-hole.

When Jo spotted the regurgitated ham, she raced around to the Websters and accused them of feeding Comet. They denied it, but she didn't believe them. Armed with a piece of wood, a hammer and some nails, Jo went up to the bolt-hole.

'How dare she block our entrance!' hissed Kiki.

Comet hung his head. It was all his fault. Kiki tried sneaking through the opening, but Jo grabbed her, pushed her to one side, then placed the piece of wood across the opening. Just as she was about to start nailing it, Sam rushed out of the house, her bowler hat askew.

'Wait, Jo. I've remembered. Comet must have eaten the ham that I left out for the magpie.'

The cats looked at each other. Jo grunted, dropped the wood, nails, then threw down the hammer. 'You should've told me before. I blamed the Websters.'

They went inside the house, arguing. Comet was about to step through the bolt-hole when Kiki nudged him out the way.

'Ladies first.' She winked then pranced into the Websters' garden.

Bill Berserk

The small town of Minton was packed on Saturday morning as people of all ages browsed around the new market. Stalls of handcrafted jewellery, used books and exotic hats and dresses lined both sides of the cobblestone footpath. Someone in a koala suit carrying a collection bucket mingled among the crowd. A fortune teller with blue streaked hair perched on a tree stump.

Jack limped over to take a look at the books. The arthritis in his right knee was giving him hell, but he was glad to escape the house. Shirl was in one of her cleaning frenzies again. He couldn't even find a quiet corner to relax without her racing around his chair with the vacuum cleaner. He pulled off his hat and wiped the sweat from his brow.

A sudden voice startled him. 'Reckon it's gonna be a real stinker today, mate.'

Jack turned to see his neighbour Ron. 'How ya goin? Didn't think flash markets were up your alley.'

Ron grinned, running a hand through his mop of grey hair. 'Norma's got the grandkids for the day, so I thought I'd get out while the going's good.'

Jack nodded. He and Shirl had no grandchildren and their only son lived in the States.

'Gee, he'll be bloody hot in that get-up,' said Ron referring to the person in the koala suit.

'Yeah.' Jack bent to rub his knee.

'You all right, mate?'

'Oh, it's just this arthritis of mine playin' up again,' said Jack.

'Heard about that new bloke who shifted into town?'

'What bloke?' Jack leaned against the used bookstall.

'You know, the one they call Bill Berserk.'

'Oh him, yeah, heard something about him being a bit strange.'

'Strange! That's putting it mildly,' said Ron. 'I went to see his thirty-acre block of land the other day and you wouldn't believe what he's living in.'

'A tree house?' Jack removed his glasses and rubbed his eyes.

Ron ignored the sarcasm. 'No, but close to it. A caravan with a bloody great hole in the roof. Says he's going to live in that until he builds a place. He's got no power, sewerage or water, except for a barrel to collect rain.'

Jack, a firm believer in life's comforts, was incredulous. 'So what does he do for a toilet?'

'He don't need a toilet. He's got plenty of bushes. Just gotta watch out for them snakes.'

The koala tripped, scattering the bucket of coins across the pavement. Several children raced to pick them up.

'So how does this guy cook then?' Jack was intrigued.

'Outside on an open fire.'

'What! In this heat, the bastard's mad. It'll only take one spark to fly and he could set the whole place alight. What does he think he's bloody doin'?'

Ron ignored the outburst. 'But Jack, you should see the bush shower he's rigged up, it's a beauty. And he's got this lunatic dog. He told me he's trained it to climb trees. This bloke's a real classic. He does up old cars, and bikes, the place is full of them. Trucks, rusted trailers, the lot. It's a real eyesore.'

'I'll bet it is.'

'He said he was short of cash, so he won't be able to get the phone on or have the power connected.'

'How much did he pay for the block?' Jack was all ears.

'Two hundred and fifty thousand.'

'Christ! Jack spluttered. 'He must be short of the full quid to pay that.'

'The best part was when he asked whether he could use my address.'
Jack fanned himself with his hat. 'What for?'

'He reckons he don't want the council to know that he's living on the land. There's some asbestos waste dumped on it and he don't want any inspectors snoopin' around. So he's going to pretend he's some kind of caretaker there and give them another address. Makes no sense to me.' Ron shrugged.

'The more I hear about this bloke, the worse it gets.' Jack's expression was grim. 'Hope you didn't give it to him.'

'Think I'm stupid! I don't want no council knockin' on my door.'

The fortune teller wandered past. She smiled at them as she undid the top button on her cheesecloth blouse.

'I reckon she fancies one of us, mate.' Ron winked at her.

'You must be kidding. Wouldn't touch her with a bargepole.'

'Bill tells me that he's gonna farm yabbies and later on he wants to build a spiritual centre,' said Ron.

This latest revelation alarmed Jack, who was very religious. 'What kind of spiritual centre?' He stroked his chin.

'Well, he told me he wants it to be a place where people can talk about their problems. He reckons he can help them.'

'Help them! The guy sounds crazy. Spiritual centre! Bet he's trying to start up some kinda cult. Minton's a quiet town, people here respect one another. We want to keep it that way.'

Ron hid a grin. Drugs and crime were on the increase and the local vicar had been charged with fraud. Surely Jack had heard about that?

'Suppose we should give the bloke a chance before we crucify him,' said Ron.

'Feeling guilty, mate?' Jack was not convinced.

The figure in the koala suit approached them, put down the bucket, then removed the koala's head. 'Phew, glad to get that thing off.' It was Bill Berserk.

Ron and Jack were speechless.

'Fancy goin' for a beer, guys?'

Madam Miss Mam

One warm spring day, Veronica ventured into a boutique. 'Do you have any fourteens, please?'

'What was that, madam?' asked the assistant, who looked no more than sixteen in a black miniskirt and ugg boots.

'I said do you have any fourteens? And will you not call me madam!'

The rowdy music pounded her eardrums. Madams managed brothels, mused Veronica. Whatever happened to being called miss, or ms? Then there was that appalling American term m'am. Now that really made her wince. What was a m'am supposed to look like anyway? A woman in lilac stockings and lace-up shoes?

'Oh, sorry,' the girl giggled, 'but you're nowhere near a fourteen. Why don't you try on a twelve? And how's your day been so far?'

Veronica ignored the question. She felt like snapping, if you must know, my husband's left me for a transvestite and my teenage daughter is pregnant to her maths teacher. Moments later, she fled into a stifling fitting room armed with several dresses all of which were much too tight.

The assistant thrust back the curtain. 'Oh, that really suits you and the colour is just perfect. It looks so elegant on you.'

How much commission was she on, Veronica wondered? She gazed in the mirror. I look like a frump. This ditzy cow knows I look like a frump. Who is she trying to kid?

Veronica handed back the dresses. 'I definitely need a larger size.'

'Oh, but madam…'

'I told you not to call me that!' Veronica yanked on her slacks.

'Sorry, well, m'am then.' She rolled her eyes and tossed her bleached hair.

'And I am not a m'am either.' Veronica flounced past the assistant.

The proprietor, a sleepy- eyed hippopotamus, guarded the cash register.

The only solution was to design her own clothes, enrol in a dressmaking course. Then at least she could create whatever styles she chose. And the best part about it would be not having to stomach being called madam or m'am.

The following week, she went to her local college, filled in the enrolment form and pointedly ticked the box Ms. No more of this madam or m'am business.

She handed the form to a staff member at the counter and as she walked away, he called, 'Excuse me.'

Veronica turned.

'You forgot to sign your form, madam.'

The Wake

She recognises me. 'Weren't we at the same primary school?'

I notice a faint bruise beneath her left eye.

She fidgets with her hands. 'You haven't changed. Still got that curly hair, freckles. Knew I'd seen you somewhere before,.' she says.

I grin, but can't place her. Amazing how she remembers me from primary. She shifts closer.

'It's not a school reunion, you two, it's a wake!' somebody utters.

We nod, allude briefly to the departed, an indoor bowler who had chronic emphysema, then we continue to reminisce.

'Remember old Heggarty, our headmaster? Wasn't he strict?' I say.

'Yeah, he sure was. Forever caning the boys – that would be seen as abuse nowadays.' She takes a gulp of wine, nibbles on a fish cocktail.

I rattle off a few more names of classmates. 'Mickey Dooley, Karen Clayton, and George Jensen. Wasn't our art teacher a lovely man?' I puzzle over his name. He used to suffer migraines, gaunt with glasses.'

'My mum worked in the school tuck shop. You should remember her?' She finishes her wine and pours another. 'Plump woman with a pageboy hair cut, always in an apron.'

'Oh, vaguely, but I rarely bought food at the tuck shop.'

'I had to help Mum before and after school in that shop, ended up leaving at fifteen got a job in a factory. It was gross.'

Was she resentful, I wonder.

She crosses her thin legs, flicks at crumbs on her blue jumper. 'My brother Craig was in your class. I was in the year below.' She adjusts the headband on her blonde hair.

'Yes, I knew him. The boy with elephant ears and a tooth-gapped smile. He was very clever.'

'Yeah, that was Craig,' she sighs. 'We used to be close. Haven't spoken in years.'

I am curious, but don't wish to pry, steer the conversation back to her mother. 'What's your mum doing now?'

'She's been dead years. I still miss her heaps.' She opens her wallet and thrusts a photo at me. 'My first grandchild, Ruby.'

A pretty toddler cuddles a stuffed toy.

'She's sweet. You must be so proud.' I hand her back the photo. 'Do you remember those Girls Brigade meetings held in that small church hall opposite our school? Did you ever go?' I ask.

'Yeah, it was fun, I loved the camps, the activities, happiest time of my life.'

'Not for me.' I pull a face. 'Too much regimentation, hated all that marching and the uniforms were horrible.' I stir my coffee.

She glances at her watch.

'Do you still live in the inner city?' I bite into my umpteenth sandwich.

'No, I left ten years ago, I'm on the Central Coast.'

'Would you like to catch up again, talk about old times?' I suggest.

Silence. She looks away. Did I say something wrong?

'Last time I arranged an outing, I ended up in hospital. I even had to lie about coming here.' She pulls up a sleeve. Her arm is covered in bruises.

My eyes stare. Mouth drops open.

'One day, I'll find the courage to leave. Look, I'd better go.' She stands, pecks me on the cheek. 'I'll always have fond memories of the Girls Brigade.'

I swallow. Watch her leave. Words choked.

Acknowledgements

Broadcasts, 4RPH Queensland Storyteller

'Deceptive' and 'Exit Left' (2007)

'The Other Half' and 'Let's Do Lunch' (2008)

'Wasp and Whistle' (2010)

'Valentino' and 'Not George' (2011)

'Something Sinister' (2015)

Broadcasts, Writers' Radio Adelaide

'Nailing It' and 'The Vestal Virgin' (2008)

Published Stories

'Prelude at Piccolo's' in *WEA Anthology* (2005)

'The Visit' in *Hot Off the Press* Anthology (2005), Women Writers' Network

'Fair Exchange' in *The Write Angle* (2011)

'Contradictions' and 'Lipstick Lullaby' in *Beyond the Rainbow* (2014)

'Friend or Foe' in *Beyond the Rainbow* (November/December (2014)

'Blackberry Blues' in *Beyond the Rainbow* (January/February 2014)

'My Man Charlie' in *Positive Words* (2016)

'Envy' in *Beyond the Rainbow* (November/December 2016)

'Mother' in *Beyond the Rainbow* (2017)

'The Reunion' in *Positive Words* (2017)

"Hide and Seek' in *Positive Words* (2018)

'Kissing Gecko' in *Polestar* (2018)